THE CRUSADERS FROM WARWICK CASTLE

Books by C. LaRene Hall

Martha's Freedom Train

Mary's Spyglass

The Crusaders From Warwick Castle

THE CRUSADERS FROM WARWICK CASTLE

A Magical Journey to the Past

Book 2

C. LARENE HALL

ILLUSTRATED BY: THERESA REYNOLDS

Idea Creations Press
www.ideacreationspress.com

 Idea Creations Press
www.ideacreationspress.com

This is a work of fiction. All the characters are fictitious, and are products of the author's imagination. Some of the events in this book did happen but not in the order or the exact same way that they are depicted in this book. Any resemblance to persons living or dead is purely coincidental.

ISBN-13: 978-0988810716
ISBN-10: 0988810719

Printed in the U.S.A.

Table of Contents

Special thanks to –

Dorthea Cook for her many ideas in writing, research, and reviewing this story.

Cindy Beck, Nichole Giles, and Tina Carney for their many hours critiquing.

Cindy Beck for editing.

Theresa Reynolds for the beautiful pictures.

Prologue

As fourteen-year-old Mary heard John enter the kitchen and grab a chair, her chocolate-colored eyes bore into him. Turning toward the computer, she made up her mind that today she would be ready for whatever tricks he played on her. As she took a sip of her milk, she heard the thump-thump of his fingers on the table, and could tell he would be more annoying than usual. *Why do brothers have to act this way?*

Mary didn't want to let him know she even noticed the irritating noise. She continued to drink her glass of milk while reading her history book, and was determined to ignore everything he did.

"Hey Sis, do you ever think about the time a few years ago when we went back to the War of 1812 to see Great-Grandpa Holt?"

Turning from the computer, she watched John getting comfortable as he leaned back on the chair, balancing against the wall with only two legs touching the floor. "I think about it often, but I don't have time for this conversation today. I have lots of homework."

"I know, but you can talk for a few minutes, can't you? It won't take long."

Mary sighed. "Don't you have anything to do?"

"Nope. I just want to talk to you. Today I thought back to the day we found that British soldier."

"I felt scared for a while, but I'm glad we helped him. Now I have to get busy. Please leave me alone." Mary gave an exaggerated sigh and turned away from John and his pale blue eyes staring at her.

When she heard the chair scrape the floor and John's footsteps behind her, she cringed. John nudged Mary as he looked over her shoulders. "Hey, you're studying the middle ages. I guess your teacher is really piling on the work, huh?"

"It's no big deal," Mary answered, closing her book so he couldn't see what she read. "In fact, I like it."

Mary wished John would go away. She knew it wouldn't be long before he would start pulling on her dark brown ponytail and making those awful horse noises. *Why does he have to be so obnoxious?*

As she searched the Internet for some new information, the familiar tug started on her head. John's talent at making animal noises amazed her and she enjoyed it when he didn't direct it at her. She gritted her teeth and tried to concentrate on the work at hand. When she could stand it no longer, she shouted, "Leave me alone!"

This outburst brought their mom into the room. "John, what are you doing? Can't you see your sister is trying to study?"

Without answering, he slipped away. Mary turned and watched her mom as she started to fix dinner. "When you have a minute, Mom, will you answer some questions for me?"

"Sure thing, as soon as I put this casserole into the oven."

Mary turned back to her book and computer, and soon her mother pulled up a chair next to her. "What do you need?"

"We're still studying the 14th century, and there's so much information on the Internet, but nothing feels right. I want to do a story about our ancestors. I'm trying hard to remember the stories you told me about our family who used to live then, but I guess I didn't listen close enough."

"For starters," Mom said, "let's go into the study. Bring your paper and colored pencils. You can draw a copy of the Thomas de Beauchamp Coat of Arms plaque that is hanging on the wall."

"It's from that time period?"

"It sure is. While you're copying it, I'll tell you a story about the Earl and Countess of Warwick Castle."

After entering the room, Mary stood staring at the plaque. "Oh, Mom, this is so gorgeous. I've never noticed all this red and gold before. My teacher will really be impressed."

"Sit here beside me on the sofa," Mom said as she patted a place near her.

"Your Great-Grandmother was Margaret Ferrers, born about 1355 to the Lord of Graby. When she was a young maiden, she married Thomas de Beauchamp. They had a son and three daughters."

Do you have any idea what all the crosses on the coat of arms stand for?"

"No, Mary, I don't. I'm not even sure what the official insignia means."

"Maybe I can find something online to explain it all."

Her mother shook her head. "That computer of yours is an amazing thing. I wish I could help with your project, but I know absolutely nothing about computers or surfing the Internet. We didn't have anything like that when I went to school."

Mary turned toward her mother. "That's okay Mom. I like doing this sort of thing. I appreciate your wanting to help, but it's something I can do."

Staring at the plaque on the wall, Mary continued to draw as her mother repeated some of the stories she had heard for years. "The Beauchamp name comes from France and it means "beautiful field."

"That's weird."

"Yeah, I think so especially since so many of our ancestors came to England with William the Conqueror in 1066. From stories I've read most of them were fierce warriors. Until the late 1850's the first born son of every Beauchamp family went into religious duty, the second born went into the army, and the third one became the lord of the lands. Many of the Beauchamp's had the title Earl of Warwick."

"How do you ever keep it straight," Mary asked.

"Usually by the wife's name," her mother chuckled. "Back in that time period women were not considered anything more than objects, but sometimes they listed the full name. It helped immensely if they mentioned the first name and maiden names. Sometimes all they said was, Countess Beauchamp. In that case, it confused me."

"I'm glad we don't have to go by a title, or there would sure be a lot more stuck-up-snobs at school."

"Maybe not. You might find yourself one of those snobs. You actually did come from noble people. Now, I really do need to go. It smells like dinner is about ready," her mom said as she stood and moved toward the door. "After dinner I have something else to show you."

"Okay. I'll be done drawing this in a minute, and then I'll come set the table."

At the dinner table, her mom filled Mary's father in on what his daughter had been doing. Mary didn't say much because she kept hoping that John would leave her alone. For some reason he wanted to be involved in her homework because he also loved history and she wanted to do it all herself.

As soon as Mary finished eating she started to clear the table. Her father raised an eyebrow, "What . . . you're helping without being asked?"

"You don't always have to ask me. I like to help and besides, Mom helped me this afternoon so I need to do something to help her."

"You're really enjoying this little project of yours, aren't you?" he asked.

"I sure am," Mary said as she started to load the dishwasher. "Do you think we could plan a vacation to England sometime?"

"Well, your mom and I have talked about it, but I'm not sure we could do it anytime soon."

"Why not?"

"It costs lots of money for a family of four to go that far."

"I could get a job."

John threw his head back and laughed. "Who would hire you? You're just a little kid."

Mary turned away from him, and worked twice as fast loading the dishwasher. *Why doesn't Dad or Mom stop him from making fun of me?* When she finished the work, she sat down next to her Dad. "I could babysit more often, and I'd give you all the money I earned. I wouldn't spend any of it on myself."

"That's nice of you Mary, but even if you babysat every day, you'd never be able to earn enough money. I'll check into prices and your mom and I will talk about it some more. I've wanted to take your mom to see the Warwick Castle where her ancestors came from. Maybe this would be a good time to consider going."

Mary threw her arms around her father's neck and gave him a big squeeze. "Thanks Dad."

"That doesn't mean we'll go," he said.

"I know, but at least you'll think about it. I'll be praying hard."

Her dad chuckled, scooted away from the table, and bent to kiss his wife. "I better get back to the farm."

"Don't stay out there working too long," her mom said as she returned his kiss.

After he left, Mary asked her mom. "Can we go to your room yet?"

"As soon as the floor is swept."

Mary hurried to the closet and grabbing the broom, she swept all the crumbs away. Hopping from one foot to the next, she asked, "Now, what are you going to show me?"

"Can I come too?" John asked.

"Not this time," his mom answered. "I think you better go outside and help your father with those animals. Make sure you get all the eggs from under those hens."

"Do I have to?"

Nodding her head Mom said, "Yes, you do."

As Mary and her mom climbed the stairs toward the bedroom, her mom told her, "I have a special treasure that has been handed down to me from your great grandmother, the Countess of Warwick."

"What is it?"

"I'll show you," she said as she opened the door to her bedroom. She walked to the dresser, pulled out an ancient looking box and carried it over to the desk in the corner. "Sit here, Mary." Mom pointed to the chair in front of the desk.

Opening the box, she removed a pin and placed it in Mary's hand. Mary gasped. "Oh, Mom. This is so pretty. How long have you had it?"

"I've had it since the day I married your father. My mom's mother gave it to her on her wedding day. It's been passed on to the oldest daughter since before the 1400s."

Mary stared at the brooch in her hand. "Will this belong to me someday?"

"Yes, I'll pass it to you on your wedding day. My mother told me that it is a *Tree of Life Pin.*"

"Mom, the branches of the tree look like arms and they are reaching out. Do you know what it means?"

"My mother told me that it symbolizes balance and harmony among the heavens and the earth."

The two sat on the bed in comfortable silence, and then Mary spoke. "You must know many stories from our ancestors of long ago."

"Yes, I do. I hope someday I can tell you all of them."

"I hope so," Mary said.

The more Mary studied about her grandparents in the 14th century, the more intrigued she became. *I sure hope that someday soon, Dad will take us to England. I can hardly wait to see all the knights, and squires. I bet John wishes he could see a real battle.*

While her mother went outside to feed the chickens, Mary snuck into her parent's bedroom to have another look at the stunning pin. She knew she had to show this to John. *Boy, will he be surprised.*

After her father and John returned from outdoors, the family sat around the kitchen table and enjoyed a dish of ice cream. Mary couldn't contain her curiosity any longer so asked, "Dad, what do you know about the coat of arms that's hanging on the wall in the study?"

"Not a whole lot. It's from your mother's side of the family. I'm proud to have it hanging there on the wall, but I haven't really paid much attention to it."

"Oh, Dad, the colors are bright. The shield almost glows because the red and gold are so brilliant. I keep wondering what those gold lion looking figures represent. There are three on the top right side and also three on the opposite side on the bottom. I drew a picture of it and I think my teacher might give me a good grade for doing the extra work."

"I'm proud of you Mary. It's always good to go the extra mile when doing your homework." He then turned toward John, "It wouldn't hurt you any, young man, if you did a little extra work in some of your classes."

As soon as their dad looked back toward Mary, John stuck his tongue out at her. She smiled and pretended she hadn't seen him. She didn't want her dad to become upset with her since, for once, he praised her for doing something.

"I do know that your mother's great grandfather was a Duke," her father said.

"Really, Mother didn't tell me that."

"I think before they moved to England they lived in France, so besides having some good old English blood flowing through your veins, you are also part French."

"Can we also go to France when we go to England?"

"I don't think we'll have time. Besides I haven't said for sure that we're going."

"I know Dad, but I'll do anything you ask me to if you'll just take us there."

"Well, young lady, you'll do anything I ask you to even if I don't take you to England."

Chapter One – The Trip

Later that year, after going through security, the small family anxiously waited to board the plane that would take them to Chicago and then across the big ocean. Mary couldn't sit still; she constantly kept jumping up and then sitting back down. She paced the window in front of the seats trying to decide which plane they would be getting onto. This was her first flight and the waiting made her nervous. "What's the matter, Sis, you scared?" John laughed.

"No, I'm not scared."

"Looks like it to me. You're the one who wanted to come and now you're probably going to run away before the plane even gets here."

"No, I'm not."

John held his sides as he continued to laugh.

"John stop making fun of your sister," his dad said.

"But Dad, look at how scared she is. It's funny."

"If you want to go on this trip, I'll not have you continually poking fun at her. You two will learn to get along, or I'll leave you here."

John slumped down into his seat and didn't say another word. He didn't even look her direction. Mary heard him mumble, "Why does he always have to pick on me. Mary can do anything she wants, but I always get the blame."

After what seemed to be many hours, Mary handed over her ticket and followed her family down a long ramp toward what she suspected was the huge airplane. After finding her seat, next to a window, her mother sat next to her, and handed her a piece of gum to chew. "The air pressure will clog your ears when we take off, so you need to chew this," her mom said.

Mary took many long breaths as the plane taxied down the runway, and then she closed her eyes as the plane went speeding away. She caught her breath as she felt the plane jerk upward.

They had all come to the airport early and Mary wanted to go to sleep but she felt too frightened to sleep on the plane. She couldn't get used to the odd noises, and every time she looked outside she only saw clouds. It just didn't seem right to not see anything below her. "Aren't those clouds beautiful?" her mother said.

"I guess so," Mary shrugged.

"You don't look convinced. Did you see that big, fluffy white one dancing just beneath the window?"

"No, I hadn't noticed it," Mary said. "I just want to see something other than clouds."

"There'll be plenty of time for that, but meanwhile enjoy the clouds. Pretend you are lying on your back at home watching the clouds roll by. You've always enjoyed seeing what shapes they make."

"But, I wanted to see the land below us."

"I know," Mom said, "but you'll be able to watch it later after we get past these clouds. They aren't storm clouds because the flight is really smooth."

Mary didn't answer, but she watched the clouds with more interest, and didn't seem so gloomy.

"There will be some turbulence," her dad had told her on the way to the airport. He didn't bother to tell her what that word meant. Mary recalled watching some airplane movies with lots of confusion, and this didn't give her any peace with all the commotion and chaos going on. This did not give her a calm feeling. As she looked at the other passengers many of them slept, others read. No one seemed upset. *Mom is right; I should just enjoy the flight.*

A stewardess brought some drinks down the aisle, and then a short time later gathered everything as the pilot indicated that they would be landing soon. Mary watched as the big metal bird hurried toward the earth. When it touched down there had been some bumps, maybe about three, and she watched as she waited for it to stop. *No way are we going to stop. We're not stopping...wait, maybe it's slowing down. Whew – that's over.*

Mary breathed a sigh of relief as the pilot said, "Welcome to Chicago."

Her mom stood and urged Mary to get on her feet. "We are going to change planes here," her mom said.

"You mean we aren't there yet?"

"No silly, didn't you hear the announcement that we are in Chicago. It's going to take us a lot longer to get to England than just a few hours."

It didn't take the family long to find the plane they needed to continue their trip. It would be a few hours until they could board so their Dad took them to a fast-food place to get something to eat. When the loud speaker announced their flight, they boarded the plane the same as before. Mary still sat with her mother, and Dad and John sat behind them. This time Mary wasn't as nervous. Now she just wished that she'd be able to see the ground below. Soon her wish came true and she watched the city lights shining and could even see little beige and green squares and circles. The headlights from the cars below formed a long stream. "Wow, that's a big traffic jam below," she said.

Mom laughed, "I told you that you'd like watching the things below."

After a while Mary couldn't see out the window any longer because it had grown dark. She slid down into her seat, and before she knew it, she fell fast asleep. She didn't stir during the long flight until her mother shook her arm, "Mary, we are getting ready to land."

"You mean the flight is already over?"

"Yeah, it is. It's morning," her mother said.

The family of four exited the plane. Mary knew that her dad had been here before because he knew exactly which direction to take, and he was always telling stories of when he was in England. Many times through the years she had wished that she had longer legs. She couldn't run as fast as anyone else could, and she always scrambled to keep up. No matter how hard she tried, they always left her behind. After collecting their luggage, they headed toward the car rental signs. "You're going to drive?" she asked.

Her father nodded his head, "How else do you think we'll get around?"

"But Dad, they drive different than we do. How will you be able to do it?"

"They just drive on the left instead of the right side of the road," he answered. "Don't worry, I drove all the time when I was here on my mission."

"How long will it take us to get there," John asked.

"We're headed to Warwick Castle first, and I think that will take us almost two hours, unless I get lost," her dad chuckled.

Mary felt tired even though she had slept all night on the plane, and shortly after beginning their long drive she was again dozing off. John punched her in the arm, "Hey, wake up, Sleepyhead," he yelled.

She rubbed the back of her hands across her eyes and blinked a few times. "Are we there?"

"We are," her mother said.

Mary sat up and stared at an impressive hotel. "Wow, this is nice," she said. "Where are we?"

"Not far from the *Warwick Castle*," her father answered.

"You mean we get to go to the castle today?" she asked.

"No, it's too late in the day to do that. We all need a good night's rest, and then first thing in the morning we'll head to the castle."

Chapter Two – The Ghost Tour

"This Ghost Alive Tour is going to be so much fun," Mary said as she grabbed John by the arm and pulled him behind her up the concrete steps leading to the door at the top of the hill.

Reading the brochure she received at the Castle entrance made her anxious to hear all the tales about the haunted tower and the restless spirit of Sir Faulk Greville. She could hardly wait to hear the story about the manservant who had murdered him.

Once a sizeable group gathered, the tour guide told them to follow him. Following close behind John and Mary climbed the stairs. After they went inside the gloomy *Watergate Ghost Tower*, Mary wondered if she only imagined the creaks, groans and mutterings coming from dark doorways as they explored the room.

"This is where *Greville* lived while the castle underwent repairs," the guide said.

The two followed the others up the flight of steps to the bedroom. Mary's imagination ran wild because she thought she heard low voices, and she could almost hear someone telling the chilling tale of the murder. *Why does it have to be so dark?* she wondered.

The inky blackness became so bad Mary couldn't see her hands in front of her nose. The tour guide told them, "While *Sir Fulke Greville* and one of his man-servants went away to London, an argument broke out between the two men. It concerned the contents of *Greville's* will. *Ralph Heywood*, the manservant, knew that his master only cared about the restoration of the castle, and would not leave him anything. When *Sir Greville* looked the other way, *Ralph* drew a knife and stabbed him. Then realizing what he had done, he turned the blade on himself and died immediately."

Mary clutched John's hand as she stumbled against a wall that opened up.

* * *

In a panic she shouted, "John, where are we?"

"Shhh." John whispered.

"Why?" she screamed. "It's dark, and I can't see anything, not even my own hands."

"Just be quiet. Someone might hear us."

"Good, then maybe they'll turn on a light," Mary said as she spoke a little quieter.

Still whispering John asked, "Did you forget where we are? I'm sure they don't have any lights here. They were only using candles."

Mary sighed and grabbed his arm as she moved closer to him. "What is that awful smell?"

"Just smells like mildew or something like that to me."

"It's sickening." Then she lowered her voice. "Where did everyone else go?"

"I'm not sure. We followed a group of kids on that stupid *Warwick Castle's Ghosts – Alive Tour*. Everyone was in front of us, then the lights went out and some girls shrieked. You started to fall, pulling me with you."

"The tour wasn't stupid, John. The scary sound effects gave me goose bumps. I loved it."

"Yeah, you're right, I liked the sounds, but the actors were kind of lame."

"No, they weren't," Mary slapped John on the arm. "I loved the way they dressed."

"Whatever," John chuckled. "I guess it was kind of funny when that zombie chased the older girl down the tunnel with a knife, threatening to eat her."

"That wasn't funny." Mary punched him, "Stop laughing. That was scary."

"No it wasn't. I guess the dry ice mist scared you too."

Mary paused. "Uh . . . not exactly. I'd have been okay if the ghosts had quit growling and hissing as they ran around in the dark"

"That frightened you?" John snickered.

Stop laughing at me, and tell me what we are going to do now," Mary said as she slid to the floor and grabbed her backpack.

"I don't have any idea." John listened to Mary unzipping her bag. "What you doing?"

Mary didn't answer, but soon John knew. "Hey, Sis, you're getting out your flashlight, huh."

Without answering, she moved the light around the small enclosure in front of her, and then she stood and felt the clammy rock wall behind her. I didn't see any doorknobs or any way out of this tiny area. Mary started to bang on the hard stones directly behind her. "Help," she yelled.

"What you doing?" John grabbed her hand and held it still. "Someone might hear us."

"Well, duh, that's the idea, big brother. How else do you plan on getting out of here if no one helps us?"

Mary yanked free from John and banged with both fists. She screamed as loud as she could, yet no one responded. Sliding once again to the dirt floor, Mary gave a loud sigh, "It's no use. I think we're stuck here."

John didn't know what to say, but soon he could feel her body shaking and he knew she was crying. He reached over, draped his arm around her shoulder and pulled her next to him. When he could tell the tears had stopped, he helped her stand and took the flashlight, "We'll find a way out," he said.

"How?"

"This is probably a secret passageway. If we got in here, there has to be a way out. I remember reading about lots of old castles having ways that the family could escape from the enemy without anyone seeing them. There are openings in the wall from almost every room that leads to a hidden tunnel. We just have to find it. Here hold this," John handed her the light and started tapping the wall with his pocketknife, first up one side and then down the other.

"What are you doing?" Mary asked.

"Shhh. Listen to see if any of the walls sound different." John continued tapping. Then he moved to the other side.

"Wait, John. Go back just a ways." Mary pointed the light to a spot he had been a few minutes before. "Right there," she said.

John moved his hand back and forth. "I think you're right."

The minutes dragged by, but then, huffing and puffing, John slid a heavy stone. It slowly creaked open a couple of inches. Mary shined the light and gasped as she saw a long dark tunnel ahead. "Come on, let's go," John said pulling on her arm.

The walls surrounding them looked deep. From where she stood, the ceiling looked as though it stood about six feet high, but as the light reached the opposite end of the tunnel the ceiling sloped and it looked much smaller. Mary hung back. "No, I don't want to go down there. How do you know it's safe?"

"Well . . . I don't know, but I couldn't find any other way out. Now come on," he insisted.

Mary drug her feet. "No, John, I'm not sure about this."

John tugged her forward.

"Wait, I forgot my backpack."

Mary hurried to the little enclosure and hefted her bag upon her back. She lingered a moment looking around before turning to follow John down the long path.

Soon the two went downhill, but Mary's short legs were no match for John's long ones. She remembered climbing hundreds of ancient steep stone steps up to the tower in the castle and knew it would take a while before they'd reach the main level. On the rough dirt path she often caught herself tripping on the rocks, but still they kept moving downward. Because of all the curves, she started to feel dizzier with each sharp turn.

Mary hated to touch the damp, musty and slimy walls, but caught herself reaching for them to keep upright. She saw all kinds of spider-webs and lots of creepy crawly things along the way. They moved so fast that she had a hard time catching her breath but John kept urging her forward. Finally, she stopped. "I have to rest." Gasping she sunk to the ground and reached for a water bottle in her backpack.

"I thought you were in a hurry to get out of here," John said.

"Not that big of a hurry. All this twisting and turning is making me shaky, and I needed a drink." Mary said as she laid her head on top of her bag.

"Did you like the story they told on the tour?" John asked.

"Yeah, I like ghost stories, but they aren't true are they?"

"They might be."

"I jumped when that squeaky door moved. It felt creepy watching the manservant as he snuck up and stabbed his master."

"Could you believe it when he turned the dagger on himself?" John asked. "It was cool the way the wailing kept going on and on."

"No, it wasn't. It was scary." Mary said, and then she asked, "How did they do all that blood stuff?"

"I'm not sure," John said. He wanted to continue to tease her, but instead said, "But it wasn't real, so there's nothing to worry about."

"Well . . . I know it's not real, I just wondered how they did it."

John shrugged and then asked, "Do you think we'll find the castle's witch?"

"I sure hope not." Mary shivered and jumped to her feet. "I'm starting to get cold, so we better get moving again."

"Wait a minute. What have you got in that bag anyway?" He reached for her bag.

"Don't you touch it." She pulled the bag from his reach. "I have a jacket in case I get cold and my cell phone if Kathy calls."

"There's no way she's going to call. I doubt she has international calling, and I know you don't."

"Well, maybe not. But remember last time we went away all my paper and pencils came in handy. You'd have starved if I hadn't brought my backpack."

Nodding his head John had to agree. "Yeah, but if you have a jacket and you're cold why haven't you put it on?"

He waited for her to pull her jacket out of the backpack and put it on. Then she took the lead and they continued the long descent, having no idea what they would find.

"I'd think we'd be at the end of this by now, wouldn't you, John?" she asked.

John shrugged his shoulders, "I don't know. It seems we've come a long ways. Why . . . do you want to go back?"

Mary stopped, "Of course not," she said. "How stupid do you think I am? The end has to be near. I can feel a slight breeze. Do you think we're almost to the end?"

"Could be, but I don't feel anything."

John made shadows along the wall from the light his sister carried. Mary pretended to not notice what he did because she knew he wanted to scare her. She continued to shine the light ahead, searching for anything that would help her get out of here. When she stopped, John almost ran into her. "Ahh . . . Jo—hn, I don't know which way to go," she said.

John stepped to her side and watched as she shined the light first one way and then another direction. "Wow . . ." he whistled.

"What should we do?" Mary asked.

"I don't know," John shook his head.

"That path goes straight ahead, and the other one keeps going down."

"I'm not going to decide. You pick."

"Well, I want to get out of here, so I think we should keep going down."

The further they went the smaller the path became. John had to follow Mary because they both couldn't stand next to each other on the narrow trail. Mary came to an abrupt stop and John looked over her shoulder. Up ahead it looked like iron bars.

Wow, it looks like a jail," John said as he tried to pass her. "A real dungeon."

"A dungeon?" Mary squeaked. "Let's go back."

John pushed her ahead, and as they rounded the corner, Mary almost ran into a guard standing at attention. "Who goes there?" he shouted, raising a sword.

Mary's voice froze in her throat and she couldn't speak. In fact, she could hardly breathe and she didn't dare move. John stopped. "We're just a couple of kids trying to find our way out of here."

"How did you get here?" the guard roared.

Mary stood still, almost in a trance. She didn't even blink. John turned and pointed back the way they had come, "From that way."

"That is impossible. The guards would have stopped you. Only prisoners and guards are allowed here."

"There were no guards," John said.

"Do not talk back to me, young man, or I will show you what happens to those who come here uninvited." The guard slowly put his sword away and reached to grab John.

Mary stomped on the guard's foot and shouted, "Run, John, run."

They ran as fast as they could, back the way they had come, through the tunnel and up the hill. Neither of them looked back. John grabbed Mary's hand and they ran until they reached the fork in the tunnel. Panting, Mary turned around and said, "I can't run any more. We have to stop and rest."

John turned around. "I suppose it's safe. I don't see anyone chasing us."

The two sunk to the ground and gasped for breath. "I thought he might throw us in jail." Mary said.

"Yeah, me too. Thanks for helping me escape. I thought you were too scared to do anything."

"I was until I saw him reaching for you." Mary laughed, "I'll bet I surprised him."

"I'm sure you did," John chuckled.

"Well, we better go find Mom and Dad before they get upset because we took so long."

"Besides if that guy isn't an actor he may be on his way to throw us in that dungeon," John reminded Mary.

Chapter Three – The Guards

They hadn't gone far before seeing a thin stream of light ahead. Mary quickened her pace, anxious to find her parents. John hurried to keep up with Mary as she ran ahead. They came to a turn in the trail and Mary slid to a stop. "Where are we?"

John stood next to his sister and starred ahead. They saw two men dressed in armor pacing back and forth in front of the entrance. Mary backed up until she turned the corner. "Jo—hn, how are we going to get past those men?"

He shrugged his shoulders, and leaned back against the stone wall. "I don't know."

Mary looked around the corner. "They don't look like they are just pretending to be guards. I think they are really protecting this entrance."

"Trade me places."

"What are you going to do?"

"I'll sneak closer and see what I can find," John said as he crept past his sister. "Stay right here."

"I'm not going anywhere," she whispered, sinking to the ground to wait.

Soon John came back. "A . . . Mary, I don't think this is the right way."

"It has to be."

"Looking out past where the guards are, I don't see any grass. All I see is dirt and then a tall wall. This is not the way we came to the castle."

Tears slid down her face. "But, there's no other way. I'm not going back to the dungeon, and I'm not going back to that little room."

John paced back and forth. Finally he stopped, "Maybe we're on the other side of the castle, the side that's near the river."

"Is there any chance getting past the guards?" Mary asked.

"That should be easy. I doubt they are real, but we had better not take any chances. Follow me," John said.

With John in the lead, and as quiet as could be, the two crept closer to the opening. They watched the two men marching back and forth and realized they didn't ever look right or left, only straight ahead. "Let's hide behind that rock," John whispered.

They stayed hidden as much as possible against the stone entryway and crept closer and closer. Mary just knew that any minute someone would yell at them. John pulled her behind a giant rock and they waited for a while. Mary kept watch around one side and John on the other side. "This isn't going to work," she whispered. "One of them is always looking this direction."

"I know." John turned and inspected the wall behind where they stood. After a few minutes, he grabbed Mary's arm. "Look behind us. If we could get high enough, they wouldn't see us as we go around to the other side. They never raise their heads to look up."

Mary turned to watch John. "How do you plan on getting high enough without them seeing you?"

"That shouldn't be too hard."

"I'm sure you know that there's no way I'm climbing up there," Mary said.

"Do you have a better idea?"

Mary sunk to the ground with her back against the rock. She peeked out at the guards and continued to watch them. "If I run fast enough when they get to the corner and start to turn, I can be in the middle and pretend that I'm lost. I don't think they'd hurt me. While I'm distracting them you can get away, and then I'll meet you down the road."

"Are you crazy?"

"Have you got any better ideas?"

"Well, yeah, it would be easy to climb up the wall. I could boost you," John suggested.

"No – forget that idea. I'm not going to try that. There has to be a better way."

"Okay, Smarty Pants, what's your brilliant idea?"

Mary shrugged her shoulders and hung her head

"Let's go back inside – there has to be some secret passageways," John said. "We didn't really look along the side walls for anything. I'd rather spend a little bit of time inspecting each section than chance those guards grabbing you. Dad would never forgive me if I didn't protect you."

"John, I had no idea you cared."

"I don't. I just don't want to be in trouble when you get hurt."

"I'm big enough to take care of myself. You don't have to watch out for me."

"I'm not saying that you aren't big, but let's do it my way this time," John said as he turned and headed back inside.

When Mary realized she sat all alone she crept from behind the rock. She really didn't want John to leave her alone and she didn't want to run from the guards. As the two approached the fork in the path, John turned right, away from the trail leading to the dungeon. He felt the wall as they steadily climbed upward. Mary followed close behind, shining her light along the wall instead of on the trail ahead. She almost ran into John because he stopped to look at the wall closer than usual. "Hey, Sis, shine the light right here."

It looked like a definite impression of a doorway, with no doorknob. John felt around and then Mary handed him the light and with her small fingers she inspected all around the indentation. "I wonder if it's a hidden entry like the one we came through earlier," she said.

"Why, what did you feel?"

"Nothing really, but when you shine the light just right, it looks like a door."

"That's what I thought. Here you take the light again and I'll find something to pound with."

"Why are you going to pound?"

"Duh, so someone can hear us."

"No! I don't want anyone to hear us. Let's just push on the door. If it doesn't work on the one side, we'll try the other one. It looks like a door so it has to open," Mary said. She put her back to one side of the almost visible door and started to push with all the strength she had.

"Did you feel that?" she asked.

"Yeah, keeping pushing little sister or maybe trade places with me and let me see if I can get it to move more."

As soon as John started to push, the doorway gave and the two went flying.

Chapter Four – Freedom

The door stopped before they could go all the way inside. "Do you see anyone?" John asked.

"No, I can't hear anything either."

"Well, can you squeeze through the opening?"

Mary sucked in her stomach and slid carefully into the room. John came in right behind her. The only light came from the beam of the flashlight. "Do you think it's nighttime?" Mary asked.

"I don't know. We haven't been gone that long, have we?"

Mary shined the light all around the room. "Maybe it's dark because of those big long drapes. They are dark and look really thick."

The two crept toward the diamond shaped windows and Mary reached her hand out and slid one curtain aside so she could look outside. Bright sunlight entered the room almost blinding them. "I guess we have only been gone a little while," John said.

"I'm sure glad. I wouldn't know what to tell Mom and Dad if we were gone all day and into the night."

John laughed. "You're such a worry wart."

Mary pushed him in the arm, "No, I'm not."

She tugged trying to get the drapes to open further, but they didn't budge. "John help me. I want to look outside."

John reached high above her head and pulled one side wider, but not far. "I wonder why they don't open more."

Mary put the flashlight into her backpack and then went to the other side of the window to pull on it there. They couldn't find anything on the side like at home to open the drapes so after yanking on each side for a few minutes decided that would have to do.

Mary flopped into a large chair next to the window. "Wow, that was a lot of work," she said.

"I wonder if this is a library – look at all those shelves of books."

Mary gasped, "Yeah, there are thousands of books. I had no idea they would have so many things to read."

John began walking around the room, pulling books out of the bookcase, flipping a few pages, and putting them back in place. Then he sat on the couch and just stared.

"What are you doing?" Mary asked.

"Nothing."

"Well, we better do something. I'm hungry and I need to find a bathroom."

"Okay, let's find a way out of here," John said. "Maybe Dad will buy us a hamburger."

Mary jumped to her feet and walked to a door. She opened it slowly and peered into the hallway. Some steps went up and some stairs lead down. Across the hall was another door. She listened, but heard nothing, then turned back toward John, "I wonder where everyone is."

John pushed the door open far enough that he could see the hallway. "What way do you want to go?"

"I still want to find food, but I don't smell anything, what do you think?"

"My guess is that the kitchen would be down. Now that we're inside we can go almost anywhere we want. That is if we don't run into any people."

"Why would that matter, there were lots of people around the castle when we went on that tour? We're bound to run into someone."

"Yeah, you're right," John said. "Just don't talk to anyone."

The two hurried to the staircase and descended the stairs. John hurriedly took the steps two at a time. Of course, that left Mary way behind. *I sure wish I were taller so I could hurry faster.*

When she reached the bottom step she heard a door slam. She looked around for someplace to hide. Behind the steps She quickly slipped inside a door behind the stairs. *I wonder where John went.*

Mary listened as a couple of people walked past the place where she hid. She couldn't understand what they said because they talked too quietly. Mary waited a long time after the voices had disappeared before she opened the door. John crouched by a window watching outside. When she came out from behind the stairs he asked, "Where have you been?"

"I heard voices so I hid myself."

"Oh. I thought they had caught you."

"Where were you?" Mary asked.

"I heard them coming so I ducked behind that chest."

Mary laughed. "I'm surprised they didn't find you. That isn't a hiding place."

"Shhh . . . someone might hear you."

"What did you see outside?"

"Nothing much. I could see the guards walking back and forth. This place looks nothing like the
Warwick Castle that Dad and Mom brought us to this morning. I wonder where we are."

"What are we going to do?"

"I don't know. When those people walked past me they were dressed way different. I don't think we are going to fit into this world."

Mary gasped. "What do you mean by this world?"

"Well, there's no one around that is dressed in jeans. All the women are wearing dresses."

"Are you telling me what I think you are telling me?"

"Probably," John smiled and then ducked his head.

"John, what have you done?"

"I don't know what you're talking about. I didn't do anything. We just went on a ghost tour. That's all."

Tears slid down Mary's face.

"I'm really sorry Mary, but I didn't do this," John said.

"What are we going to do?" Mary asked between sobs.

"I'm not sure, but maybe we better go upstairs and see if we can find some clothes. At least if we look like these people maybe somehow we can get away from them."

Mary nodded her head and turned toward the staircase. She climbed the spiral stairs slowly until she heard someone coming in through a door. Then she ran as fast as her little legs would go. She didn't even stop to see if anyone was in the room across the hall from the library, but charged in with John right behind her. She closed the door and leaned against it catching her breathe. Inside pink linen curtains were pulled back, revealing a beautiful large bed with a heavy wooden frame, covered with a pink frilly quilt, and lots of pillows. "Jackpot," Mary said. "This is a girl's room."

"It sure is," John turned and opened the door. "After I find some men's clothes I'll come find you. Stay here," John commanded.

Mary quickly slipped over to a wooden chest sitting across from the bed. She pulled open the drawers and looked inside. Beautiful fabric filled the drawer, but no Levis or shirts or anything looking familiar lay inside. She couldn't even find a dress. She picked a beautiful piece of linen material and pulled it out. Holding it up, she could tell that the tunic covered her okay, and would probably fit like an oversized t-shirt. After removing her clothing, she pulled the fabric over her head, and tried to figure out how to tie it securely. She certainly didn't want it flapping open. Satisfied with how she looked, and the way the clothing fit, she hid her own clothing under the bed.

Then she started to pace the floor. The only other furniture in the room was a stool. Looking at her feet she wondered if she needed to find something different for her feet. With that thought in her head she started to look for something else. She only found some slippers. She kicked off her shoes and scooted them under the bed. Then she sat on the stool to pull on the slippers. *That's better*, she thought.

She peeked outside the door, but saw nothing. Since she didn't know which direction to look for John she stayed in the room, but she went to the window and peered outside. Now she knew why John seemed concerned. The people walking outside were dressed in clothing like what she had just put on, except the women had something on their heads. It looked like a veil and hung loosely. Mary left the window and began searching the room for something to put on her head. She found nothing that she wanted to try.

When John slipped inside the room. Mary, stifled a laugh. "Well, look at you," she said putting her hands on her hips and walking in a circle around him.

"Don't you dare laugh. I don't look much different than you anyway."

Mary nodded her head. "You're right, you are dressed almost like me, but the material I have is much nicer."

"Why would I want to wear girly looking stuff like that?"

"You're right. The tunic you have on looks just right for you. Where did you find those stockings?"

"It's what all the men are wearing," John said.

"I know, you actually look like those men outside, but those pointy-toed shoes are sure funny looking."

"You mean you've been looking outside. I hope no one saw you," John said.

"No one looked up at me, but if I hadn't looked I wouldn't know that I need to find a veil to cover my head."

John helped her look around the room, but couldn't find anything to help. "Well, you'll just have to go like you are," he said.

Mary agreed and then said, "Let's find something to eat. I'm starving."

Chapter Five – Finding Food

Mary opened the door and after looking around to make sure the coast was clear, she slipped into the hallway. John followed close behind. They went down the stairs in search of a kitchen or food. After looking inside a couple of rooms on the next floor they descended further down some more steps. At the bottom, they turned toward a delicious smell and found a kitchen full of women working. John started to turn away when someone saw him and called, "What is it you want, young man?"

"My sister and I are hungry. We were looking for something to eat."

"The food isn't ready yet. Did you sleep in again?"

John shook his head and turned to leave. "Wait just a minute," the servant lady called to him. "Here are some berries, and then you can go out to the well and get you something to drink."

"Thank you," John said as he reached for the offered food.

"That won't even start to fill me," Mary whispered as the two left. "I wonder how soon we can get something else to eat and where we're supposed to go."

The two found the door leading outside and John cautiously pulled it open. Now that they had dressed properly, they didn't have to be as careful when they saw other people. It didn't take them long to locate the well and find a drink. "I'm sure glad that all we have to do to get a drink is turn on a faucet," Mary said.

"Yeah. That's much better, but this water isn't so bad, and it's cold."

After taking a sip of the water, Mary asked, "Now, where do you think we can go to find food?"

"The only place I know that we can find some food is probably back in-side the castle," John said laughing. "I doubt there is any other castle nearby."

"Very funny, Big Brother."

Before heading inside, the two stood and looked off into the distance. As far as they could see, many different animals and wide-open land covered the landscape. "I wonder what they are growing over there," John said as he pointed toward a large hill.

"I'm not sure," Mary said. "Maybe after we find something to eat we can go exploring."

"Sounds fun to me."

Although they saw lots of people around, the two acted as if they knew what they were doing and went back inside to look for the dining room. They saw a few other people and followed them, all the time pretending they knew where they were going. They followed the people through a large brass door and found themselves inside a giant room.

Wide-eyed Mary slowly twirled around. "Wow, this is a big room. I bet it's the largest room in the castle, but the floor is only dirt covered with straw. John, why do you think the walls are lined with carpet, but there is none on the floor?"

John shrugged his shoulders. "I have no idea, but I think we found the right place. It looks like someone has been eating and drinking in here," he said.

"You're probably right."

Mary enjoyed observing the unique room. "Look up there," she said, pointing to the high ceiling with a loft. "And look at the narrow white-greenish glass windows."

"Hey, look at these wooden shutters. It looks like they are secured by an iron bar," John said pulling Mary nearer.

"Why do you think it's so dark in here?" Mary asked.

"That's obvious. They don't have clear glass like the windows at home. There's no way any sunshine could get in through that green tint."

John grabbed Mary by the hand and started pulling her to the center of the room. "You have to see this stone fireplace."

"It smells awful," Mary said as she held her nose and coughed.

"I don't think there's anywhere for the smoke to escape."

They both stood and stared at the smoke rising through a lantern-like structure in the roof. Mary thought it looked like someone pulling strings, similar to those on the venetian blinds at home.

John gazed around the room and then poked Mary in the arm. "Hey look at that," he said reaching for a huge cauldron. "This looks real old."

"Yeah, it does, almost like something a witch would use."

"It looks like they've been cooking stew in it, probably to feed all the men that I've seen around here," John said looking inside the pot.

Aisles with benches just like at church ran the full length of the room, and rows of wooden posts supported the timber roof. In front, of the benches were tables covered with white cloths, and filled with lots of food.

"Let's go find a place at one of the tables. I'm starved," Mary said.

It didn't look like anyone had any particular place to sit so John and Mary sat next to some other young people. They kept a low profile while at the table, and didn't talk to anyone else, hoping no one would talk to them. These people really had a strange accent, and Mary knew she couldn't pull that off no matter how hard she tried.

Not sure what to do, they both watched those around them. Mary noticed a pewter spoon at each place, but no forks. She watched as the people at their table took a sharp pointed knife from a sheath attached to their belt. Since she didn't have a belt she didn't know what to do for a knife. Mary pointed to the people with the knives. John shrugged his shoulder, and the two pretended everything would be okay.

Directly in front of them sat a mug filled with a sweet smelling drink. John held it to his nose and turning to Mary he said, "I think it's probably alcohol."

"Oh, no, what will we do?"

"Just leave it alone."

Along with the drink, there were apples, and some crackers, cheese, and olives. Being hungry Mary ate a little bit faster than most of the people at their table. Next, bowls were passed to them with cabbage, chicken and broth. After that came pork and other vegetables, some nuts and a pear. John and Mary didn't know what to do when after eating another drink was passed their way. This time they knew for sure that the spicy smelling drink was some sort of wine. They again set the drink aside. "I'd sure like another drink of water, or a glass of milk," Mary said as she wrinkled her nose. "This stuff smells awful."

They were both full and relieved when everyone started to leave the table. "Now, what do you think we do?" Mary asked John.

He shrugged his shoulders. "Let's just follow everyone else for a while and see what they do during the afternoon."

He started walking, pulling Mary with him. "Don't you think we should try to find Mom and Dad?" she asked.

"Mary, they aren't here. Don't you understand that we are in a different century? We left them back at the castle."

"What century are we in?"

John shook his head. "I'm not sure. The clothing isn't like anything I've ever seen, and the food is different. You were studying about medieval time, maybe that's where we are," John said still shaking his head.

"But I want to go home," Mary said as a tear slid down her face.

"Oh come on, Mary. It won't be that bad. Let's enjoy this while we can. When we get tired of this we'll figure out a way to go home."

"No, John. I'm scared. What if we can't go home?"

"I'm sure there will be a way to go. There's nothing to worry about."

"That's what you always say, but last time there was a war all around us. What if there's another war?"

John gulped and didn't say anything.

Mary stopped walking. "You know something that you aren't telling me, don't you?"

John ducked his head. "Well, remember, we're in England. Right?"

"We were when we got sucked into the wall," Mary said.

"In history last year we talked about a hundred-year-war."

"Hundred-years?" Mary exclaimed.

"Yeah."

"John, while we were eating some of the kids talked about a war. What do you know about that?"

"If I remember right, the immediate cause was Edward III of England being upset with Philip VI of France for not fulfilling his pledge to restore a part of Guienne taken by Charles IV. The English wanted to control Flanders because of their wool and other cloth. Phillip supported Scotland instead of England.

"And they fight about this for one-hundred years?"

"That's right," John answered. "But, I'm sure there's other problems also. I just know that the war inflicted lots of misery on France. Their farmlands got ruined; they had famines, and also the Black Death plague. They say that with the ruins of the war an entirely new France emerged."

"I don't agree – nothing good can come from a bunch of men fighting each other," Mary said.

"Oh, I'm not sure about that. I sure wish while we are here we can watch a real battle, especially with the English Army. I've heard that they form a formation with two triangular blocks of archers standing on either side of dismounted men-at-arms creating a funnel which is difficult to break down. Since our army doesn't use archers I would like to watch such a battle."

"Well, I hope you don't get your wish. I really don't want to watch any fighting going on, even if it is just with bows-and-arrows.

John turned his head so Mary couldn't see his smile. He knew she had no idea how deadly those archers could be.

Chapter Six – Exploring

The next morning Mary and John crawled from the hard bed they had found in the stables. Mary had a hard time getting all the straw from her hair, and didn't know what to do about her rumpled clothing. John just slicked his hair back with water from the well, and then declared it time to eat.

After breakfast they wanted to go exploring, but first they had to get past one of the two entrances – the north or west walls. There stood a wooden drawbridge over the moat with steep sides in the North-east and in the centre of the north-west wall stood a gateway with towers on either side. As Mary looked back at the castle she believed that the residential part of the castle lined the eastern side of the castle, facing the river. Also along that side of the castle, Mary knew the great hall, library and bedrooms they had been in yesterday stood.

The first thing Mary noticed was the river she had seen in the distance, but along the way, she also saw the beautiful fields with the pale blue flowers. "I've never seen anything like this at home," Mary said.

"I think that's because we don't grow any of these plants."

"Why not?" Mary asked.

"I think they're grown in the east."

"What kind of plants are they?"

"I think they're called flax, and some of its hemp. It's an important fiber for clothes."

"Like cotton?"

"Well sort of, but more like linen, and the oil is used as a wood preservative."

"How come you're so smart?"

"I just read a lot and sometimes I watch the Discovery Channel."

In the first field they came to the hay and Mary watched several men and women using rakes, and also large forks with three prongs made of wood. Others stood up and used a long-handled tool (scythes) that they cut something with. They had to hold it with both hands and it looked like they used a slicing action.

In the next field, Mary and John watched as a horse pulled a harrow used to break up some of the soil and cover up the seeds. It looked like it had four beams, into which was set some wooden teeth. The beams were joined together by some wooden crossbeams. As the two continued walking, they saw a plough making a deep furrow and turning the earth. To get the right depth for the seed the plough had to cut and turn the earth. John bent down and felt the clay soil. "I'm sure glad that I'm not working in this field," he said. "It's not easy to work with clay dirt."

Closer to the river John stopped to watch some men with a wooden spade. "It looks like they're digging a ditch," John said. "I'm sure glad we don't have to do it that way. Our modern equipment is much better. Dad usually uses a plow. When it has been raining the wheels become clogged with mud, but it's sure easier than digging with a shovel."

John and Mary came to the edge of the cliff and searched for a path going down to the river. "Do you know the name of the river?" Mary asked.

"Yeah, I read on the castle brochure that its name is Avon. Dad told me that it's over 96 miles long. There are lots of little streams that flow into it."

As the two neared the river, they noticed a large working trebuchet siege engine. "As the arm is lowered," John explained, "the rectangular bucket full of rocks is raised getting ready for the throw. When the trigger mechanism is released, the weight of the rocks in the bucket pulls the base end of the arm down and the opposite throwing end accelerates up and over the top, throwing the rocks right down the field."

Mary enjoyed watching John's actions as he explained the interesting machine to her. John continued. "The trebuchet is capable of hurling huge rocks considerable distances and can batter castle walls repeatedly during a siege. Eventually the wall of a castle can be breached enough to allow attackers to fight their way inside the castle."

"But why is it here?" Mary asked.

"So if someone tries to attack the castle they are prepared ahead of time for battle to fight the enemy."

"But I thought they weren't fighting right now," Mary said.

"Well, they aren't, but they have to be ready."

As they approached the riverbank, Mary noticed an island. Downstream she could see a mill, but no bridge to take them to the island. Mary knew she could get there without much trouble. She took off her slippers as she collapsed onto the grassy riverbank. "What are you doing?" John asked.

"I'm going wadding."

John gasped. "But . . . what if someone sees you? You can't do that."

"Why not?"

"Well, maybe they don't do that sort of thing in this country."

"How would you know anything about that," Mary said as she stood and put her hands on her hips. "I don't know any of these people, and I don't care what they think. I'm going wadding, and while I'm at it, I'm going to go over to that island," she said pointing downstream.

With that, she pulled the tunic above her knees and put one foot into the water. She quickly pulled it out. "Wow, that water's cold."

She put it back into the water and then stepped with the other foot into the river and started walking toward the middle of the river. "Oh, this feels so good. You ought to come in John."

"No way. I'm going to keep watch for other people heading this way. If I see someone coming you're going to get out of there."

"Nope, I'm not. A whole pack of horses couldn't pull me out of here until I'm ready to get out."

John paced awhile and then walked up the hill so he could watch Mary who continued to enjoy the refreshing water as she trudged downstream. Once in a while, John would call down to her, telling her to hurry, but each time she called back, "I'll get out when I'm good and ready to."

Finally, she reached the little island. She walked onto the bank and looked around. On the river bank some geese waddled around, and nearby a raccoon sat on a log watching her. Just as she started to go a little farther she noticed a herd of deer. Not wanting to disturb them, she held perfectly still. Mary could hear John calling her, but she didn't answer.

After enjoying the peace, Mary decided she better get back across the river to where John was still waiting. He was going to be so mad, but she didn't care. Once on the other side of the river she stepped out of the water, grabbed the slippers, and headed to the spot where John laid waiting for her. "Did you have fun?" John asked.

Mary gave a big sigh and nodded her head. "It felt wonderful."

John started to walk back toward the castle and Mary had to hurry to keep up. "Slow down, what's your hurry?"

"Well, we've been gone a long time."

"It's not like anyone is going to miss us," Mary said.

"Yeah, you're right," John said as he slowed his pace. "What do you think we should do for the rest of the day?"

"Maybe we could go snooping around. I'd like to find a place where we can sleep in a bed tonight, or maybe if we go around to the other side of the castle we can find Mom and Dad."

"That's not going happen, Sis."

Mary wiped a tear off from her cheek with the back of her hand, and kept walking. John slowed and grabbed her by the arm. "It's going to be okay, we'll find them."

Mary shook her head and tried to pull away from him.

"I'm sorry. We'll walk around to the other side of the castle right now," John said as he pulled her along.

"What about the guards?"

"Don't worry about them. With us dressed like this, we fit right in. They'll just think we belong here."

Mary watched all the people they passed working in the fields. Occasionally someone would wave, but no one tried to talk to them. John led her away from the door they had originally come out of and kept pulling her around the castle. "Who do you think all these people are," Mary asked.

John shrugged, "I'm not sure. My guess is they are servants because everyone seems to be busy and no one is even looking at us or wondering what we are doing."

They passed by many stairs and doors that led inside, but John kept moving forward. Mary kept watch all around her. She knew that at any moment someone would stop them. They kept walking and walking. "John, stop."

"Why?"

"Well, I think we are just going in circles. Everything looks the same."

"That's not possible," John said.

"But look back there," Mary said pointing to a doorway. "That's the way we came out earlier today."

John did stop, and he looked toward where Mary pointed. "Yeah, you're right. That is the way we came out." John turned around and then turned back again. "I don't understand. Nothing changed. Did you see the path we took to go on the ghost walk?"

Mary shook her head. "No, I didn't. There weren't any such paths. Now what are we going to do?"

"Yesterday we took a cement sidewalk, not this dirt path. I've not seen anything like that here. Let's take that doorway and go inside and see what we can find in there," John said as he took Mary by the arm.

Mary followed John inside. After going through the room where they had eaten earlier, they opened a doorway into another hall. They wandered up and down several hallways, but they only found more rooms. Then they climbed some stairs and found more rooms. Mary found the room where she had left her clothes, but decided to leave them safely under the bed for now. "Maybe we should go downstairs," John said.

"No way," Mary stopped walking. "I don't want to go anywhere near that dark dungeon."

"Maybe after dark it would be a bit scary, but during the day time we should be okay."

"Ah . . . John, we were there in the day time, during the morning. Did you forget already?" Mary asked.

"No, I didn't forget. I just wanted to tease you. Do you have any idea how to get to it from the courtyard?"

"Why would I want to do that?"

"Well, I think it's in the heart of the main courtyard. I doubt that it's that bad. I'm sure they just made things up to look frightening on the tour. They probably have lots of bloody bodies lying around, maybe some torture implements or better still maybe they are showing how they execute someone. I think they do anything they can to scare people."

"John, do you think you're making me feel better about this by telling me all that stuff?" Mary asked.

"Well, I guess not, but if we stay close together we can watch out for those dark sinister things."

Mary slugged John in the arm. "We are not going anywhere near that dark creepy dungeon. So just forget about it and drop the subject now."

"But, all we're going to find up here is more bedrooms. Let's just go down a little ways. You and I both know that the dungeon is way down. If we just go one floor below where that giant hall is, we won't be anywhere near the prison. Okay?"

"One floor will just take us to the kitchen, so I'm willing to go that far."

Mary started going down the steps, and passed a couple of girls running up. The girls turned to look at Mary, but they didn't say anything. Mary kept walking, and had to resist the urge to run. She didn't want to have to talk to anyone. After a few steps Mary turned to watch the girls and could see them eyeing her brother. One girl whispered to the other one, and then they both broke out in a laugh.

"What's that all about?" John asked.

"I think they think you are cute," Mary answered.

John turned bright red, but didn't say anything. They continued descending the stairs and soon arrived one floor below the large room. In the long and narrow hallway they could hear lots of commotion. "What do you think is going on?" Mary asked.

"If I didn't know better, I'd think lots of people are on the other side of those doors, making food. I can smell something cooking and it's making my stomach growl."

Mary walked over to a door, and carefully opened it a crack. "You're right," she said as she again closed the door. "I don't want to go in there, or they might put me to work."

John laughed. "Could you tell what we are going to be eating for dinner tonight?"

"Nope."

"Ah, come on, Sis. Tell me what you saw."

"Okay, but you'll be disappointed. They were cutting cheese."

"Really?"

"Yeah, I'll bet this level is the servant working area and maybe their quarters. If we don't want to be in their category, maybe we better get out of here."

"Okay, the next time we see steps going up we'll leave."

As they wandered the halls they never did find anything of interest. "Tomorrow we're going to explore outside," John said.

"But we did that today."

"I mean we are going to look around those big round towers out there. Or maybe we'll leave the castle and explore the surrounding villages."

"Okay. That sounds fun," Mary said. "Do you think it's almost time to eat?"

"All you ever think about is food," John said.

"I know, but let's go back to the large hall and see if there's anything to eat yet."

"I'll race you," John challenged as he started to walk faster.

"That's not fair, you already got a head start."

Once inside the room they realized they were just in time. Several people turned to watch them enter, and a nice couple indicated they should sit at their table. The first thing passed around was a tomato broth. After eating that, they were handed some chicken wrapped in smoked bacon topped with a puff pastry. Then they had some potatoes that tasted like thyme. For dessert they had a cherry and apple crumble served with cream. It surprised Mary that they had such great food to eat, and she had enough to eat long before they stopped passing the food to her.

Chapter Seven – The Search

"Hey, do you think maybe we could find Great-grandma's bedroom?" John asked.

"Do you really think that we are back in time to our great-grandparents era? I never thought about that, but maybe she is here."

"To me, it looks like the right time period, and since you just studied about this time period in school its possible."

"You're right. No wonder so many things look familiar," Mary said.

"I remember when I studied about the medieval time period I wished that I could live then. It always looked so exciting and my secret dream was to be a knight on a huge black horse."

Mary laughed. "You a knight? Unbelievable."

"It could have happened if I had been born about six-hundred years earlier."

"So, how do you think we go about finding her bedroom?" Mary asked.

"My first guess would be that the chambers for the owners of this great place would probably be on the second floor."

"But we already looked around that area," Mary said.

"I know, but after a few doors we stopped looking. Maybe we need to search all the rooms."

"That would take a long time."

John nodded his head. "Yeah, it would take a long time, but what else do we have if we don't have lots of time?" John chuckled and continued, "We could split up."

"Oh no you don't," Mary stomped her foot. "There is no way you are leaving me to search anything on my own."

"Okay, calm down, I only wanted to tease you."

Smiling Mary said, "Now let's go up to the second floor and start where we left off earlier."

John grabbed Mary by the hand and then the two of them almost skipped up the stairs. Mary's excitement grew because now they had a purpose. They had a reason to look into all the rooms.

The first few rooms they looked into seemed way too small to belong to someone as important as a countess, although some of them were beautiful enough. Next they peered into a huge room, but it had a definite masculine design. "Wow," John said. "This is great. I could live here forever. There's a desk, and chair across from the bed."

"Yeah, John, but there's no TV or video games. There's not even a computer. You'd never survive here," Mary said.

"You're right," John sighed. "I'd be bored in a few hours without those gadgets. Even the trip has been a little boring since

Dad wouldn't let me bring my laptop. I can't even search the Internet."

"At least he let you bring your IPod so you could play some games. What did you do with it anyway?" Mary asked.

"It's right here in my pocket," John said as he reached for his pants. "Whoops, I forgot I had to take them off when I pulled these ridiculous stockings on. Maybe we better go find our clothes."

"I'm sure mine will be okay," Mary said. "I pushed them under the bed. What did you do with yours?"

"I think I just left them in a heap on the floor."

"You're right, we better go find them," Mary said as she left the room and headed the opposite direction from where they had been searching. "Hurry, John."

"What's your hurry? They aren't going to get up and walk away," John said.

"I know, but maybe someone found them. Maybe they'll keep them, and then what will you do?"

It only took a few minutes for them to find the room where John had left his clothes, and just as Mary thought, they were gone. John put his face into his hands and sunk to the floor, letting out a loud moan. "What am I going to do?"

Mary didn't know what to say. She just stood still watching, and then she went into action looking under the bed and in every nook and cranny she could think of. "Mother is going to kill you John if you don't find those jeans. She might not care about the shirts, but the pants cost lots of money."

"You don't have to remind me, I know."

"Well, are you going to just sit there in the middle of the floor moaning or are you going to help me look for them?" Mary asked.

John came to his feet and almost tore the bedroom apart looking for his clothes. "Why me? I really wanted to use my iPod."

"That's the least of your troubles. Why did you just leave them sitting on the floor?"

"I didn't think," John answered.

"Obviously. Well, since your clothes aren't here, I'm going to make sure mine are okay." Mary left the room and hurried down the hall. After opening the door to the bedroom she had used, she gave a sigh of relief. Her clothes were right where she had left them. She crawled under the bed and pulled everything out. She shoved her clothes into her backpack and decided to take everything with her. Never again would she just leave the bag behind. It didn't matter if it made her look different, someday it might come in handy.

She went back to the other room to find John. When she entered with her backpack he didn't look happy. "Looks like you're not going to be in trouble."

"Yeah, isn't that great," Mary said.

"Sure. Who do you think took my clothes?"

"I think that maybe some servant picked them up. Maybe they took them to wash – if you check back later or tomorrow maybe you'll find them."

John nodded his head. "You're probably right. I guess that's all we can do here for today. Let's get back to looking for the countesses' bedroom."

The two hurried back to where they had stopped their search and went to the next room. "Bingo!" John shouted.

Mary peeked inside and was surprised when she saw a magnificent bed more elegant than anything she had seen today. She felt like claiming the bed for her own because it looked so comfortable. "Even back then, they knew what girls liked."

"Mary, she isn't a girl."

"Same thing – you know what I mean."

John laughed. "Yeah, I know. I just wanted to tease you. Do you think she keeps that pin in here?"

"I doubt that. She probably wears it, and it isn't a pin, it's a brooch."

"Whatever."

Mary walked around the room, but didn't dare touch anything, afraid of disturbing it and someone finding out she had been in the room. John noticed her hesitance and told her, "If you don't touch anything how can you tell if it's here."

"But if I touch someone will know."

"That's silly," John said. "I'll look for you."

Mary moved toward the door and watched John as he looked inside drawers and on top of tables. Finally, he shook his head. "It's not here."

"Maybe it's not even her room," Mary said.

"I'm sure it is, but if you want, we can keep looking."

The two left the room and looked inside all the rooms, as they wandered around. When they came to the stair's John motioned for them to go down. Mary followed him, not sure where he would lead her. Then he wanted her to go down the next flight of stairs. Mary paused for a minute and then followed him. She didn't want to be left alone. Once on the lower level, she grabbed his arm. "Where are we going?"

"I think this is the floor where the servants are, so I thought we'd see if we could find the washroom. Maybe my clothes are still there."

"Good idea," Mary said.

Several times they passed some girls carrying clothes or food. Mary looked into a large kitchen. The food smelled delicious and her stomach growled letting her know it was getting near time for the evening meal. Everyone kept busy and paid no attention to a young girl watching them. She realized John had left her behind so she hurried to catch him. "Did you smell that food?"

"That's all you ever think of is food."

"I know, but I'm still hungry."

"That last girl we passed carried an armload of clothes. She came from this direction, so I'm sure we're getting close," John said.

Mary nodded in agreement and the two continued down the hallway. John opened the door to the next room and stopped. "Look – there is a scrub board. Let's go inside this room," John suggested.

Mary followed him. "Do you see your jeans?" she asked.

"Not yet."

"Keep looking, they have to be here somewhere."

John looked and looked and then stuffed in the very back of the room behind a large bucket he saw them. "Here they are."

"Well, grab them and let's get out of here."

"But they're wet," John said.

"So. At least now you have them."

"But . . . where will I put them?"

"Don't look at me," Mary said. "You aren't using my backpack. I don't need all of my stuff getting wet."

"Then what will I do?"

"You're the oldest you figure it out," Mary said.

John surprised himself as well as Mary. He pulled up his tunic and hurriedly put those jeans on. He didn't want to lose them again. He reached inside his pockets, but they were empty. "Oh no, Mary, my IPod is gone. Now what am I going to do?"

"Even though you found your Levis, I think you're still in trouble."

"Well, help me find it," John said.

The two searched the entire room, and still didn't find the IPod. "Maybe the servant kept it," Mary said.

"But if she did, wouldn't she be afraid the person whose clothes she had would report her?"

Mary shrugged. "Maybe."

"Maybe the girl we passed returned them to the room. We have to go back there and see if she returned it, or find the girl and ask her what she did with it. I just have to have it Mary. Dad will never buy me a new one. Besides how will I ever explain to him what happened?"

Hurrying down the hall they found the girl. "Hey, I saw you earlier," John said.

Mary kept quiet. She knew she could never fake any sort of accent and didn't want anyone wondering why she was here.

"I have not seen you before," the servant girl said.

"Yes, you came out of that room," John said pointing toward the room, that they had just exited.

"What do you want?" the girl asked.

"When you washed my jeans you found something in the pocket."

"Yes. I found something, but what do you mean jeans?"

"Never mind. What did you do with my IPod?" John asked.

"I put it in the room," she said.

"Thank you," John said as he grabbed Mary by the hand and took off on a dead run.

Slow down," Mary hollered. "I can't run that fast, and besides you'll draw lots of attention if we don't just walk."

"You're right," John said. "We do need to be careful, but can't we at least walk fast?"

"Okay."

As they approached the room, they saw a young man enter the door shutting it firmly behind him. "Now what are we going to do?" Mary asked.

"I don't know, but I'm going to get my IPod back," John said as he pounded on the door.

"Yes, what do you want?" the young man asked.

"I left something in your room," John said.

"What were you doing in my room?"

"Just changing my clothes. Can I just get my IPod?"

A handsome, dark haired young man stepped aside and let John in. Mary hung back, she didn't want to go inside. "You can come in also," the young man said.

"No thanks," Mary said.

"My name is Richard," what is your name?"

"I'm Mary, John's sister."

"It is a pleasure to meet you," Richard said.

"I'm also glad to meet you," Mary said.

"Please come in," Richard said.

"No thank you. I'll wait here in the hall for my brother."

"Will you be having dinner with us this evening?" Richard asked.

"I'm not sure," Mary answered.

"Please do. I would be honored if you would sit with me," Richard said.

"Can my brother sit with us?" Mary asked.

"Yes. That would be nice," Richard said.

Just then John pushed past Richard and came into the hallway. "Found it," he said.

"See you at dinner," Richard said as he bowed to Mary before closing the door.

"What was that all about?" John asked.

"He invited me to dinner."

"What?" John stopped walking and turned to Mary. "You can't have dinner with him. You aren't old enough to date."

"Why not? I'm hungry and we have to eat, and it's not a date."

"Okay, but you better be careful," John said.

Chapter Eight – Meeting the Earl and Countess

When John and Mary entered the great hall, they were astonished because everyone dressed in their finest clothes. "I guess we should have dressed up," Mary said.

Richard stood up and immediately walked toward Mary taking her by the arm. "I am glad that you would join me for dinner," he said.

John followed behind the couple, and sat next to Mary. Richard introduced both Mary and John to several friends, and to his sisters; Katherine, Margaret and Elizabeth. Mary smiled at each of them and then after looking around the room for a few minutes she pointed to the front of the room, and leaned in to talk with Richard.

He smiled. "My father, the Earl's table is raised on a dais at the front of the hall." Richard then told them that the guests are arranged by social standing. "Since you are my guests you can eat at the same table as I do. The lower classes are required to sit on the far side of the salt cellar," Richard explained as he pointed to the other side of the hall.

The conversation around the table was friendly. When the meal began they passed some scones and a bowl of broccoli broth around the table for each person to fill their own bowl. Next were plates filled with smoked salmon and asparagus tartlet with a lemon dressing.

When Mary had finished eating the food, she started to get full. She watched as servants brought platters of roasted breast of chicken covered with a honey and mustard glaze. There were also bowls with butternut squash and sweet potatoes with a creamy garlic sauce. Next they passed a bowl of thyme potatoes and a rustic summer salad. This time Mary only took small portions of each thing offered.

By the time the servants brought the dessert of apple and nutmeg sponge with custard Mary felt ready to explode. It smelled delicious and she had always been a big fan of dessert, but she only took a small spoonful. Richard looked at what she had taken and tried to encourage her to take some more. "No, everything tastes great, but I'm full and doubt I can even eat this small portion," she said.

After dinner they were entertained by musicians seated in the loft, overlooking the hall. Other entertainers roamed the hall juggling, and doing acrobats, and singing.

Katherine leaned over and whispered, "These men are troubadours that my father hires.

"Do they do this every night?" Mary asked.

"Not always, they travel around a lot to all the castles in the area. I love it when they come. The singers are my favorite, especially when they sing songs of love."

When the four had finished eating Richard took Mary by the arm, and said, "I want you and John to meet my parents."

Mary protested by pulling her arm away. "I don't think that's a good idea," she said.

"Why not?" Richard asked.

"We're not important people," John said.

"That does not matter," Richard said. "You are my friends, and my parents always want to meet those I associate with."

"But, we're not royalty," Mary said.

Richard laughed. "Most of the people here are not royalty. That does not matter."

Mary let Richard take her arm again and obediently followed him to the front of the great hall. "Mother, Father, this is my friend Mary, and her brother John."

"I'm pleased to meet you," Mary said as she moved forward to shake his mother's hand.

His mother stepped back a couple of steps, "Nice to meet you, Mary."

Mary then turned toward her father, "Good to meet you, sir."

Richard's father nodded his head. Then John moved forward and tried to be friendly by shaking each of their hands, but they both just stood there watching the two children. Richard leaned toward Mary and whispered, "It is proper to bow."

Mary turned bright red and stammered, "I didn't know."

Then Mary tried again, "Pleased to meet you," she said to Richard's father as she curtsied.

Richard's father laughed. "Where are you from Mary?"

"Utah, sir."

"Where is that? I have never heard of that place before."

"A . . . it's a long ways away, clear across the ocean."

"No wonder you talk so different. How long have you been here?" he asked.

"Just a little while," Mary answered.

"Well, welcome to our castle. My wife, the countess, and I are happy to meet you. Any friends of Richard's are friend of ours. Are your parents here?"

"No, sir, they couldn't come."

"That is too bad. Well, make yourself at home here and if we can help in anyway please ask."

"Thank you, sir. What should I call you and your wife?"

"I am Thomas De Beauchamp, the 12th Earl of Warwick, and my wife is the Countess of Warwick."

Mary gulped. She almost couldn't breathe. These were her great-grandparents and she couldn't even tell them. She turned her attention to the countess and smiled as she noticed the beautiful brooch fastened at her neckline. "That's a beautiful pin," Mary said.

The countess reached to touch the brooch and nodded, "Thank you Mary. My mother gave it to me, and her mother gave it to her. It is very dear to me."

The three children excused themselves and exited the large room. Once they were in the hallway Richard pulled the two to a stop. "John, earlier you said that you left an IPod in my room? What is an IPod?"

John ducked his head. Finally, he looked up. "It's just something that I use to pass the time when I'm bored."

"I do not understand, what do you mean when you are bored?"

"When I don't have anything else to do, then I can pull out my IPod and I can play some games."

"Will you show me?" Richard asked.

"Sure," John said as he pulled it from his pocket."

"What are you wearing beneath that tunic?"

"Just my clothes. I actually borrowed the tunic from your room so that I would look like the rest of the people," John answered.

Richard laughed. "You look so funny."

"No, I don't. It's you that looks funny. It's stupid running around in a girl's dress all day."

Mary tried to slip away from the arguing boys, but Richard caught her hand, "No, you stay here," he said turning back toward John. "These are not girl's dresses. This is what all of us wear," Richard said. "But I want to know what you are wearing beneath it. Show me."

John pulled up the tunic to reveal his pair of jeans. "What kind of material is that?" Richard asked.

"Just Levi material. All the boys wear them back in Utah."

"You never really told my father where this Utah is. How far away, and how did you get here?"

"It's a long ways and we flew on an airplane," John answered.

Too late John realized his mistake as Mary punched him in the arm. "John isn't there something or somewhere you need to go," Mary asked.

"Oh yeah, please excuse me," John said as he ran down the hall.

"What was that all about?" Richard asked.

"Uh . . . nothing, I just needed to remind him about something," Mary answered. "This is really a beautiful castle. It's the first one that I've ever been to."

"Really? This is where I was born, and there are many castles nearby," Richard explained.

"What year is it? Mary asked.

"1397. Why do you ask? It should be the same year where you live," Richard answered.

"Yeah, of course it is, I just couldn't remember," Mary said. "What do you do all day?"

"Mostly I work in the field with the servants or practice with the knights. Father believes that everyone needs to do their share of the work."

"Yeah, my mom and dad make me do a lot of work also. We live on a farm, and have lots of animals to take care of," Mary said. "There are lots of fields where we grow hay, an apple orchard, a barn where we keep the cows and horses, a chicken coop, and we also grow a garden. Our house is nothing like yours, it's just a small place compared to your home."

"I see. Do you own the farm?"

"My father does," Mary said.

"Let us go find your brother, I still want to see that IPod of his."

"Okay," Mary said hoping that John hid in a good place.

"Where will you be staying tonight?" Richard asked.

"I'm not sure, we hoped to find our parents and go back to the hotel with them."

"Where are they?"

"I don't know. John and I left them so that we could go on this cool ghost . . . we wanted to see the castle. Since we went inside we haven't been able to find them."

"How did you get inside? Usually the guards do not let any strangers in," Richard said.

"We didn't see any guards."

"That is not good. I better go tell my father about that. He will not be happy to know that the guards are not protecting the castle any better than that. With the war going on, this is not good news. Please excuse me," Richard said as he turned to rush from the great hall.

"What war?" Mary asked.

"I will explain later," Richard said.

Mary hurried down the hall hunting for John. She went upstairs and still she couldn't find him. "John," she called over and over. Mary looked inside Richard's room, and all the other rooms nearby. Then she went up the next flight of stairs. Still she couldn't find John. She went out to the stables where they had slept last night, but she still didn't find him.

Finally, she went back inside and found a quiet dark place beneath the stairs and sat on the floor. *John and I are really in a mess. I don't know what to do. How do we explain about John's clothes, or about the IPod. There is no way we can tell Richard about the airplane. He'll think we're crazy. I wonder what Richard meant by a war going on? I have no idea where to find John.* With so many thoughts rushing through her head she lay down and cried herself to sleep.

Chapter Nine – The Feast

The next morning Mary awoke with a start. *Where am I?* she wondered. Then the prior evening came rushing back to her. *Oh, no. Where will I ever find John. He promised he wouldn't leave me alone.* She rose to her feet and decided to go downstairs and search for him again. Her stomach rumbled and she also knew she needed to find some food. *I wonder if I can find something to eat downstairs where all the servants hang out.* She kept going down the stairs until she knew it was the right floor, then she started walking toward the good smells coming from the kitchen. She walked inside and stood watching the girls at work. Finally one of them looked up, "What can I do for you, Miss?" she asked.

"I wonder if I can eat down here instead of upstairs?" Mary asked.

"No, Ma'am, no one eats in here, you will have to go eat with all the other guests."

Mary turned around and walked back the way she had come. She climbed the stairs and casually walked to the huge room. She wondered if John would be there, but didn't want to get her hopes up. She opened the door and looked around. She felt relieved that she didn't see anyone she knew and she found a table in the corner and sat alone. A servant brought her some food which she scooped on to her plate and ate quickly not even noticing what she put into her mouth. She hoped that she could get out of there before anyone noticed her.

As she left, Richard caught her arm. "Where have you been?" he asked.

"Nowhere, just hunting for my brother."

"You mean you have not seen him since last night?"

Mary shook her head and then a tear slid down her face.

"May I be of service?" Richard asked.

"No, thank you, I'll find him," she said as she wiped the tear away with her arm. "See you later."

Richard grabbed her arm, "No, do not go. Let me help you. I have lived here a long time and I know all the good places to hide."

The two walked toward the towers outside. "My father wants me to go with him, but my mother insists that I am too young to go this time," Richard said.

"Where is he going?"

"I am not sure, probably to the King's Palace. It must have something to do with the war."

"Are you talking about the 100-year war?" Mary asked.

"I am not sure. I do know that it has been going on for a long time."

Whoops, Mary thought, *I've opened my big mouth again. I wonder if I'll ever learn.*

Trying to distract Richard, Mary said, "So where are we going to look for John? Last night I looked in all the bedrooms."

"If that is the case, we should go outside. There are lots of buildings out there where he could have hidden."

Mary followed Richard as he led her outdoors and toward some of the buildings. After searching a few, Richard suggested they go to one of the towers. "That's a good idea," Mary said. "John noticed them yesterday and I'm sure he wanted to go inside."

Richard grabbed her hand and the two ran toward the first tower. "Do you really think John would come here?"

"Yes," Mary said. "He was upset because we didn't have time to come here earlier. He loves anything to do with fighting and wars. I guess he's a typical guy."

"Well, this tower has been here a long time. It is pretty small and not the best place to be during a battle."

"Why?" Mary asked.

"The small space makes for hard working conditions and the noise is awful. When someone fires a cannon, there is nowhere for the noise to escape. I think many soldiers have probably gone deaf because of that awful noise. My father always makes me leave when they are going to fire the cannons. He says that the smoke from the flames smells awful, and it is too dangerous for a young lad like me. Some men have had their faces burned during the explosion."

"Oh, how terrible."

As they approached the tower, they decided to be quiet and surprise John if they found him inside. That way he wouldn't have a chance to run away. They crept inside and climbed the stairs being careful they didn't make any noise. Sure enough, almost to the top they spotted John lying in a pile of straw, sound asleep. Mary hurried to his side, and reached down to shake him. John came awake with a start. "How did you find me?" he asked.

"It was not hard," Richard said. "Yesterday you ran off before you could show me that gadget of yours – I think you called it an IPod."

"I'll show it to you, but it won't do any good because it doesn't even work here."

"Why not?" Richard asked.

"I don't know, but you can see for yourself. When I turn it on, nothing happens," John handed it to Richard.

Richard just stared at it. "Well, you have to turn it on," John said.

Mary reached over to show him the button. When she pushed it, nothing happened. "You're right John, it doesn't work. It must be just like my cell phone. There's no Internet service here."

"What are you talking about?" Richard asked.

"Oh no, I've done it again. Never mind, Richard, you wouldn't understand," Mary said.

"Since I can't show you how the IPod works, what is there to do around here?" John asked.

"We could play chess," Richard suggested.

"You mean you know how to play chess?" John asked.

"Sure I do. I have been playing since I was a tiny little chap."

"That won't be any fun," Mary said. "Only two can play at a time. What will I do while you two are playing?"

"We could go fishing down at the river," Richard said.

"Okay." Mary and John both shouted at once.

Their time at the river went much too quick for Mary, she had hardly thought about her parents at all. Before she knew it, the servants had come summoning them back to the castle with news about a big feast to be held that night. On the way, Mary hung back. Seeing how reluctant she acted Richard also stopped. "What is the matter," he asked.

"I'm a little nervous. I really don't have any other clothes to wear and I don't know what to do."

"My sister Katherine has lots of clothes. I will have her help you," he said.

"But, what about John?"

"Do not worry about him. I will take him with me. You will both have a great time at the feast. There will be many important people there, and besides eating, we will be dancing. I can hardly wait to dance with you," Richard said.

Mary felt worried. From the things she had studied in school, she knew there wouldn't be any shuffle dancing at this dance like there was at her school. Her parents would be upset if she went with Richard because they didn't think she should date until she was at least sixteen. Maybe they could just go as friends.

Richard took her to his sister's room and knocked on the door. "Katherine will you please help Mary find some suitable clothes for the festivities tonight. Help her to look her best. I will come and get her after John and I are ready."

Katherine seemed to be a little older than Mary, probably more like 16, but Mary hesitated to do much talking. She knew she spoke different from Katherine who had a definite British accent, and Mary spoke like a small town girl from Utah, so she didn't ask many questions. Katherine was a giggly girl, and laughed a lot while trying to see what she had that would look good on Mary.

"How old is your brother?" Katherine asked.

"He's almost 16," Mary answered. "Do you have any other brothers?"

"No more brothers, but you met my two sisters. Your brother is very handsome," Katherine said. "Is he promised to someone?"

"Lots of girls like him, but we aren't allowed to date until we are sixteen. How old is Richard?"

"He turned sixteen at the beginning of the year. What do you mean by your parents do not allow you to date? Most of us girls are married by the time we reach the age of fifteen or sixteen," Katherine said. "I am sure glad I do not live where you do."

"Why?" Mary asked. "I wouldn't want to marry at such a young age."

"I am looking forward to marriage. I would not want to be a spinster."

"Most of the girls where I live wait until after they have gone to college to worry about getting married. They date and get to know lots of guys before they settle down to get married."

"College?" Katherine asked.

Whoops, "That's school," Mary answered.

"You have to go to school before you can marry?"

"No, we don't have to, but most girls want to go."

Katherine shrugged her shoulders, "Well, if you are anxious to get to know lots of men, you will love the party," Katherine said. "All the knights from nearby castles will be here."

"Maybe I shouldn't go. I wouldn't know how to act," Mary suggested.

"No, you have to go. Richard probably will not like it, but you will get to meet many good looking men from all the neighboring castles," Katherine said.

"But, I'm only fourteen," Mary protested.

Katherine laughed. "That is the best age to start looking around."

Long before the girls were ready, the boys knocked at their door. Once the girls were dressed in the finest clothes Mary had ever seen, they went with the guys down the spiral staircase to the Great Hall below. When Mary entered the hall, she caught her breath. The room looked more beautiful than she could have ever dreamed. There were centerpieces in the center of each table, and large four feet banners lined the walls. In each corner of the room were lighted torches.

"This is amazing," Mary said.

"You look beautiful," Richard told her.

Mary ducked her head. She felt her face turn warm, and she didn't know what to say. No guy had ever complimented her before. She didn't want this kind of attention. What could she do? She slipped her hand from his and turned around to look for John. He looked deep in conversation with Katherine, and didn't even glance her way. Mary watched him for a few minutes and then decided to interrupt him.

"John, can we talk for a minute?" Mary asked.

"Sure, Sis. Katherine, please excuse me."

"Wow, aren't you the polite one."

"Mom has always taught us to be polite so what's the problem?" John asked.

"Mom has also taught us that we aren't supposed to date until we are sixteen, so what are you doing?"

"I'm not dating. I'm just talking to a nice girl."

"I know, but John did you forget that we are in a different century. You can't get serious with this girl," Mary said.

"I'm not serious with her I'm just talking to her. What's wrong with that?"

Mary shrugged her shoulders. "John, I don't know what to do. I don't want to like Richard and he keeps coming on to me. I've never gone out with a guy before and I don't know how to act."

"Oh, that could be a problem. You are still really young. What do you want me to do?" John asked.

"For starters, don't leave me alone with him."

"How am I going to stop you from being alone with him?"

"You could just stay right next to me all night. Don't let him give me any hugs, okay?" Mary asked.

"Katherine is going to think I'm a creep."

"That doesn't matter what she thinks. After this trip you aren't going to ever see her again."

"Yeah, you're right. I'll try to watch out for you," John promised.

John pulled Mary with him over to where Katherine stood. Every time they moved he made sure Mary stood right beside him. Both Katherine and Richard seemed a little perturbed by their actions, but they both insisted that they had to stay together. "We don't know anyone else here," John explained to Katherine. "She's my little sister and I have to watch out for her."

"But Richard will not let anything happen to her," Katherine protested.

"I know, but Mary's a little shy and hasn't ever been with a guy before. She's a little bit nervous, so let her stay with us. Okay?" John said.

"Richard is not going to like this," Katherine said.

Mary smiled and moved closer to John. Richard tried to grab her hand, but she moved to the other side of John. Mary felt relieved when the time to sit down to eat arrived. She had to sit by Richard, but John sat on the other side. Mary knew the meal would be more elegant than the one the night before.

For starters, they were served some yellow split pea and potato broth, followed with garlic and thyme roasted chicken, butternut squash and sweet potato parcel with creamy garlic sauce, as well as minted potatoes and a rustic salad. Everything tasted delicious and melted in Mary's mouth. She never dreamed that food prepared in the fourteenth century could be so great. Deseret included a ginger sponge with custard and a cheese platter accompanied with biscuits, pickles and celery.

After the meal, the foursome roamed the great hall visiting with other young people along the way. Finally, some men started to play music. Richard immediately asked Mary to dance. "I've never been to a dance before. I only know how to dance one way," Mary said.

"That will be alright. I will dance the same way you do," Richard said.

Mary doubted that would work, but nodded and started to dance. Richard took a few steps, then stopped and watched. After many minutes, Mary felt everyone watching her and she came to an abrupt stop. *Oh, no! I've done it again. Not with my mouth this time, but with my actions. I guess no one here dances like this.*

"What kind of dance is that?" Richard asked.

"It's the way we dance in Utah," Mary answered.

"I think that my parents will think that kind of dancing is a little wild."

"I'm sorry, maybe you should show me your way."

"My pleasure," Richard said as he took her hand into his. "We have only been able to dance like this for a few years. Now follow me. Sometimes couples form a processional formation, and sometimes they form a long line and hold hands. Take one step forward and a second step to bring the feet together. Or if we do a double we take three steps forward and the fourth step to bring the feet together."

"That sounds easy enough," Mary said.

"Now we are doing a sashay and everyone is going to form a circle and we will face inward and hold hands. We will step sideways to the left."

It didn't take Mary long to catch on to the dance and she enjoyed it because it kept Richard's attention away from her. Richard taught her several dances. One of them they called arming, where they gripped each other's elbows with one hand, and used two doubles to walk in a circle.

Mary enjoyed the night, but dreaded for it to end. She was afraid that Richard would try to kiss her. He was serious about her and it scared her. She knew that John wouldn't understand her feelings because he only wanted to make fun of her. Oh how she needed her mom nearby where she could ask her questions and tell her the way she felt. *Oh, Mom, where are you?* Mary silently called.

Soon the dancing concluded and people started to leave. She looked around the room until she found her brother and Katherine. Without waiting for Richard, she moved toward the two. "Hi, you two. I wondered where you were," she said as she approached them.

"Hi, Sis," John called. "Thought we had lost you."

"Well, I know you tried to, but it didn't work," Mary said grabbing John by the arm. "I wanted to go with Katherine to her room. She told me earlier I could sleep there."

"But, I think you could find your own way," John said.

"No. I don't want to go alone," Mary explained.

"You go ahead and go up," Katherine said. "I will come along later."

Mary had no other choice so she hurried away to the room, and was grateful that she never saw Richard along the way. No way did she want him trying to kiss her. She didn't want that kind of relationship. From what Katherine had said she knew the girls married at a very early age. She would keep her distance from Richard from now on.

Quietly Mary snuck into Katherine's room. She felt around in the dark until she found her backpack under the bed. Then she pulled one of the fluffy pillows from the bed and crept to the other side of the room and found a corner far from the door. She removed the fancy dress, and slippers and laid them on the stool. She then tried to make herself comfortable. Inside her bag, she found a jacket and covered herself with it. Mary hoped that she would be asleep long before Katherine came.

She heard someone knock on the door, and she held her breath until she knew they had moved on. The dancing had totally worn her out, so it didn't take long for sleep to overtake her. When Katherine came, Mary slept soundly, and dreamed of running away from this castle. A knight dressed like Richard chased her.

Chapter Ten – The Sabbath Day

When Mary woke up the next morning, Katherine was putting on her best clothes. "What are you doing?"

"Today is Sunday and after a quick meal, we are going to church. I assumed that you would want to go."

"Of course, I always go to church. I never miss a week," Mary answered taking extra care to make sure she looked her best. Her mother didn't let her wear makeup yet, but she did have some lip gloss that she carefully applied to her thin lips, and she brushed her hair a few extra strokes hoping that her hair would shine. She missed the lavender shampoo that she always used at home. When she asked Katherine what she could use to wash her hair with, Katherine pointed to the huge bar of soap. No way could Mary use that stuff on her body, let alone on her hair. She wondered what they used to keep their skin soft or maybe that didn't matter to women in the fourteenth century.

"Is the church that building that I saw near the stables?" Mary asked.

"That is a church, but we also have a chapel here in the castle."

"Oh. I didn't know, I've never seen it," Mary said.

"It is down the hall from the music room."

"Why aren't we going to the church over by the stables?"

"My father is still having work done on St. Mary's, Chapel of Our Lady. His father had the Gothic stone construction done before his death, but my father is still continuing the work," Katherine said. "My grandfather's tomb is in that church."

"I remember reading about that on the Internet. Also someone named Richard De Beauchamp has a tomb located at the center of the Beauchamp Chapel."

"There is no Beauchamp Chapel," Katherine said. "And, I do not know of a Richard that is buried in the church. What is the Internet?"

Whoops, there I go again talking about things that will happen in the future. "I'm sorry," Mary stammered. "It's just something I use at home to find information."

"I love hearing about things from your world. Are you almost ready?"

Mary nodded and headed to the door. "I'm really hungry."

The two girls joined the boys for breakfast and then they headed toward the chapel. It wasn't anything spectacular, just a simple small room with an altar at the front. "This is the nave," Katherine said. "We stand here to listen to the priest preach."

Both John and Mary nodded and stood next to Richard and Katherine. After the short services John asked Richard where the priest stayed. "He has a room in the top of the tower, over there," Richard pointed. "I do not know how much Father has to pay him to stay here and preach each week, but I do know the servants take food to him a couple of times a day."

"What are we going to do now?" Mary asked.

"Since you asked about St. Mary's church let us walk over there and take a look around," Katherine suggested. "I will certainly be glad when we are able to attend church there. It is a magnificent building."

The four strolled past the stables and over to the entrance of the church. Inside John and Mary stood in astonishment. Mary turned around and around looking at every little detail. "I have never seen anything this spectacular in my life."

"It is certainly impressive," John said nodding his head. "Very impressive in deed."

"It takes my breath away," Mary said.

They explored for a long time, and then Katherine asked, "Are you almost ready to go home?"

"Yeah, we can do that. It's probably time to eat anyway," Mary said.

On the way to the castle, Mary couldn't stop talking about the fantastic church. "We have nothing in comparison back home."

* * *

After the mid-day meal the four retreated to their own rooms. Katherine picked up some stitchery, and went to sit in the garden. Mary grabbed her backpack and tagged along. Once in the garden she looked inside her bag and pulled out a book.

"What are you going to do?" Katherine asked.

"I'm going to read my scriptures."

"I wish I could read."

"I thought you did read," Mary said.

"Yes. But only a little and I have no books to read."

"But there is a whole library full of books. Don't you get to use them?"

"I doubt there is anything easy enough for me to read."

"I'm sorry. I don't have anything easy either, but after you tire of sewing we could work on your writing," Mary said.

"I would like that," Katherine said picking up her embroidery.

Mary read for about an hour and then shut her book and put it into her bag. "I'm tired of reading. Are you ready to write now?"

"Sure let me finish sewing this one spot."

Mary wandered around the garden waiting for Katherine. She admired the many birds, particularly the peacocks. She had no idea they had any such birds in England during the 1300's.

It didn't look like they could stay outside much longer because a storm definitely would be upon them soon. When Katherine called to Mary, pointing at the sky she suggested that they go inside to work on the writing. They didn't want to be cooped up in their room all day so choose the library where they worked at a cherry wood desk. Mary scanned the many shelves lined with books. Opposite the desk, Katherine sat in an overstuffed chair in the reading area. The girls easily entertained themselves until dinnertime. Mary enjoyed this peaceful Sabbath day and she hated to see it end.

Chapter Eleven – The Enemy

Mary slept late, and was surprised to see light streaming in through the windows. Katherine still slept on the bed nearby, and so Mary pulled the tunic and slippers that she had worn the day before on and carefully left the room. Her stomach growled and she wanted something to eat. She didn't want to go looking for John, or she knew she'd find Richard also. Already a plan was forming in her mind to get her and John away from this place. The only problem with that idea meant if they left, how would they find her mom and dad?

After finding something to eat, she wandered outside. She went into the stable where they kept the horses. Mary loved horses, and wondered if maybe she could take a ride. She went in search of someone to ask, but found no one around so she decided she better leave the horses alone for now. As long as she stayed safely inside the walls she knew it would be okay to stroll around the grounds. One good thing about living in this century meant plenty of open space. Things here were much greener than at home. *I wonder if they get lots of rain. They probably do, or it wouldn't be so green.*

Near where she supposed the kitchen inside would be, Mary noticed another garden with fruit trees and vines at one end, and a plot with herbs. The thing she liked most was the beautiful flowers – roses, lilies, violets, poppies, daffodils, iris, and gladiolas, as well as many that she didn't recognize. Mary wondered if they realized that the chickens were in the garden. It would make her mother angry if the chickens ever got anywhere near her gorgeous flowers. Oh well, after only a few days of being here, she knew their ways were different from hers.

Mary decided to sit alone near the beauty of the garden and think things through. There had to be a way to get back to her parents. Her first thoughts were, *How did we get here? Answer – through that stupid wall. The one that isn't here anymore.* Next question, *Why?* Mary shook her head. *I don't know.* She shook her head again and looked all around. *Not once did I wish to see my great-grandma. I didn't read a journal. I didn't do anything to cause this. Why am I here?*

Mary jumped up and started pacing back and forth. She stomped her foot and got ready to have a real tantrum and then she saw John. He hurried toward her and she met him part way. "Where have you been?" John asked.

"I couldn't find you, so I came out here to think."

"So what are you thinking about?"

"I'm trying to figure out why we are here," Mary said.

"Oh, is that all. I thought you had something important to say."

Mary put her hands on her hips and glared at him. "Why are you so obnoxious?"

"Because you're my sister," he laughed.

"Let's go for a walk while we talk about this," Mary suggested.

"That sounds okay to me."

The two headed toward the river because they thought it would be quiet and not many people would be there. They walked along enjoying each other's company, and they both splashed in the river and chased after one another, but they didn't reach any conclusion as to why they were here.

They walked together and then all of a sudden they heard the shrill panic neighing of a horse, followed by a flurry of hooves approaching rapidly. They both ducked behind some rocks and watched as bushes smashed and then the horse burst out of the trees into the open. The solid midnight color made them both stare. The sight of that beautiful horse took Mary's breath away. It had a long mane and tail that flew in the breeze. It wore a bridle and saddle with saddlebags slung on each side. The dangling stirrups and the metal fittings of the bridle were silver and the saddle looked like it was made of leather.

The horse raced past them so fast that its momentum carried it over the edge of the hill. It neighed again and panicked as it lost its balance and tumbled downward. John chased after it, but Mary stayed put. She watched John wet his finger, and hold it up to test the wind as he approached the horse. Their father had taught him that back on the farm. Mary could tell that John stood downwind because the horse had no idea John was nearby. One-hundred feet farther, crouching low Mary watched John draw nearer to the horse. She could tell he studied it and then she noticed what he had seen. Weapons; a long bow, and a six-foot lance hung from the saddle. That's all that Mary could see.

She saw John crouch down and crawl along the bottom of the hill toward the tress where the horse now stood. She watched the horse rear back as John approached it in the rear. As it came down on all fours, its hind legs dug in as it got ready to bolt. John reached the horse as it reared again but he grabbed the bridle and pulled himself up.

That was the last she had seen of John. He and the horse flew down the path away from her. Mary started to run, but as usual, her short legs didn't get her very far. Finally, out of breath she sank to the ground and decided to wait for John to return.

It seemed a long time, but finally Mary could hear the neighing of a horse and hooves approaching. She hid in the deep grass and watched in the distance hoping to see John. As the horse approached her, she could hear John, "Mary! Mary! Where are you?" he called.

She stood up and startled both the horse and John. The horse reared back, and John slid off. Then the horse took off at a fast run. "Why did you do that?" John asked.

"I heard you call me, and just wanted you to see me."

"Yeah, but now you've scared the horse away. There were some saddlebags with flint, and steel and a good hunting knife."

Mary hung her head. "I'm sorry. I didn't mean to scare the horse away. Maybe we can find it again."

"I doubt that," John said. "He is spooked. It won't be easy catching him."

"We probably need to look for mom and dad again. Besides I'm hungry."

"Well, you'll just have to be hungry, because I'm not leaving until I find the horse."

The two started to walk. John wouldn't wait for Mary. His long legs took him farther and farther from her. She felt upset, and just let him leave her behind. *He'll be sorry if I get lost. That'll teach him to walk so fast.*

Mary kept walking. Up ahead she saw something alongside the path. As she approached she saw John hunched over the horse. She stooped down beside John and asked, "What's wrong?"

John didn't even look up. "You killed the horse."

"No, I didn't."

"Yes, if you hadn't scared him he wouldn't have run off so fast."

"John, horses run like that all the time. Something had to have happened to it. I didn't do this."

John sobbed and ignored Mary. She looked around and grew frightened when she saw a bunch of men a short distance away. "John, there are some men over there watching us."

"What?" John asked.

"Don't look now, but there are men watching us."

"Why would they be doing that?"

"I don't know, but I don't think we are safe here," Mary said while looking all around. "We are almost to the castle."

"Thank goodness."

"John, do you think that maybe the men hurt the horse?"

"I hadn't thought about that. I just thought it had collapsed because it had run so fast," John said running his hand over the horses' side, and then he moved it toward the horse's neck. Stuck just below the horses' neck a long arrow was buried. "You're right

Mary they did shoot the horse with their bow and arrow. I'm sorry I accused you."

"What are we going to do?" Mary asked.

"Our only chance might be to run for it. They probably won't be expecting that. Run in a zigzag pattern, not straight. Are you ready? Go."

They both took off as fast as they could go. At the drawbridge Mary almost fell, but John grabbed her elbow and pulled her faster. The guards inside watched the approaching men and soon guards were everywhere. Thank goodness they knew Mary and John and let the two pass to safety, but the men behind them weren't as fortunate.

Chapter Twelve – The Countess and Her Brooch

That afternoon before time for dinner, Mary went in search of Katherine and soon found her in the garden she loved about as much as Mary did. "Hi," Mary called as she approached. "Have you got a few minutes to talk?"

"Yes, please come and sit by me."

Mary made herself comfortable before plunging in. "Is there any way that I could talk with your mother in private? Every time I see her she is surrounded by so many people, that I'd feel awkward interrupting."

"Why would you need to talk to my mother?" Katherine asked.

"Oh, it's nothing important. I would just like to get to know her better. She seems like such a grand lady," Mary said turning away.

"Is something the matter?" Katherine asked.

Mary shook her head and turned back toward Katherine. "I've never met a countess before, and that brooch of hers is out of this world."

"What do you mean, out of this world?"

"Oh . . . I keep forgetting that I speak different than you. It just means that it's real special."

Katherine nodded her head in agreement. "I think the best time to really talk with my mother is after the evening meal. The men usually sit around drinking and talking and mother usually goes to her room to relax before bed time."

"But . . . "

"Do not worry, I will arrange it," Katherine interrupted. "Mother has a sitting area in her room, and that will be the perfect place for you two to talk."

"Okay. That sounds good," Mary said. "I really appreciate your help."

Mary turned to leave, but Katherine grabbed her arm. "Please stay, and talk with me. Tell me about your home."

"Well, there's not much to tell. We live on a farm, out in the country, but the town isn't far away."

"What is a town?" Katherine asked.

"I think it's the same as a village is to you.

Katherine nodded, "I am sorry I interrupted you, go ahead and continue."

"Our house is really small compared to this large castle. The great hall where we eat is larger than our entire lower level," Mary said.

"Are you a servant?" Katherine asked.

Mary shook her head, "No, we are free and have our own house."

"What does your father do?"

"My father is just a farmer," Mary answered. "He raises lots of cows, and plants wheat and hay."

Katherine nodded her head again. "So you are rich?"

Mary laughed, "No, we aren't rich, but we aren't poor either. John and I help my dad when we can, but we both go to school."

"School?"

"Yeah, don't you go to school?" Mary asked.

Katherine shook her head. "No. What do you do at school?"

"Well, that's where we go to learn how to read, write, and math." *Oh, oh, I think I goofed again. How am I ever going to explain this to her?*

Katherine shook her head again. "Mostly we girls are taught to sew, and sometimes a little bit of cooking. It is not important for us to learn to read and write, but we still have lessons sometimes. What is math?"

"It's adding and subtracting numbers and stuff like that."

This time Katherine nodded her head. Finally Mary had said something that made sense to her friend. "I think I should go see what John is up to," Mary said.

"Are you coming up to my room to get ready before we eat?" Katherine asked.

"Yes, that would be nice." Mary said as she started to walk toward the castle. She changed her plan as soon as she noticed Richard walking ahead of her. Mary turned and hurried back toward the garden where she almost ran into Katherine.

"Did you forget something?" Katherine asked.

"Uh . . . Could you show me the rest of the garden? I've seen the flowers, but the vegetables and herbs really interest me."

"Yes I could, but I thought you needed to find John."

"I decided that could wait awhile. I really am interested in seeing more of the garden. "

"I am sure that our garden is like the one back at your home. There is the usual colewort, leaf beet, parsnips, and turnips," Katherine pointed at several rows of vegetable.

"No. I've never heard of colewort or leaf beet. Which ones are they?" Mary asked.

"That first row is the colewort," Katherine said.

"That looks like cabbage to me." Pointing to another row she said, "We do grow beans and peas, just like the ones you have here."

The two girls roamed the garden talking about the familiar and also the things Mary had never seen. "I really hate those parsnips. Your servants really grow lots of different things."

"The servants help with the garden, but mostly my mother works out here. She is the one who wants a little bit of everything. Over there," Katherine pointed, "is her herb garden.

Mary walked over to the other garden. She recognized the thyme and mint, but most things were not familiar to her. Katherine pointed out the rosemary, tarragon, and fennel flower. Mary was surprised at the large variety growing in both gardens. No wonder the meals tasted so good, they had plenty of spices and such a large assortment to choose from. At home her mom used spices that came in small bottles that were stored in the cupboard. Next they wandered under the trees – apples, pears, plums, cherries and peaches. "We have these types of trees at home," Mary said. "What kind of tree is this?"

Katherine came over to where Mary stood and reached to the ground. "This is a chestnut," she said handing a small nut to her.

"I've always wondered what they looked like," Mary said.

The girls spent the biggest part of an hour wandering around and talking about the different things in the garden. Mary hated to see the pleasant afternoon end, but they both realized the time to prepare for the evening meal had arrived.

Once in Katherine's room Mary asked to wash up. "I don't think we have time to take a bath," Katherine said. "But in the morning we could put the wooden tub out in the garden and you can wash up then."

"Okay. I could wait until then, except I really need to wash my face. Do you at least have a wet rag that I could use?"

"Yes, I will get one for you and show you how to get it wet."

After washing her face, Mary pulled her hair down and retrieved a brush from her backpack. She bushed it a hundred strokes and then put the brush back into her bag. "What is that bag you have your things in?" Katherine asked.

Mary gulped, and then proceeded to show the bag to Katherine. "It is called a backpack because you can put it on to your back and take it with you everywhere you have to go."

"May I see it?"

"Sure," Mary said as she handed it to Katherine.

"How do you open it?" Katherine asked.

Mary unzipped the bag and Katherine examined everything inside. Then she started pulling things out of Mary's backpack. "What are these?" she asked.

"Oh, they are for clipping your finger nails," Mary answered.

"What do you call them?"

"Just finger nail clippers. They are really easy to use. Hand them here and I'll show you how."

Katherine watched in fascination. "Does that hurt?"

"No, not at all."

"What is this?" Katherine asked as she held up Mary's cell phone?"

Oh no! What have I done? Mary thought. "That is my cell phone." Mary didn't know what else to say. She didn't like to lie and had no other answer.

"How does it work?"

"Here, I'll show you," Mary said as she took the phone from Katherine. Mary turned her cell on, but nothing happened. "I guess I don't have any service," she said.

"Service?" Katherine asked.

"Yeah, I guess my phone doesn't work while I'm here. I probably have to be home before it'll work."

Katherine held up the brush. "What is this made of?"

Mary shrugged her shoulders.

Katherine next took out the flashlight. "What do you do with this?"

Mary turned the switch and showed Katherine the stream of light that came from it. "How did you do that?" Katherine asked.

"All you have to do is push this button up or to turn it off you push it down."

"I like this. Where did you get it?"

"At the store," Mary answered.

"What is a store?" Katherine asked.

I never knew it would be this hard to be in a different century. What am I supposed to say? Mary shrugged and said, "Shouldn't we be getting ready to go downstairs?"

"Yes we should. We can talk about this later. I have the perfect dress for you to wear tonight. It is not as nice as the one last night, but we are not going to a party so it should be just right."

Katherine showed Mary how to put the dress on and then the two of them descended the spiral staircase to the hall below. She caught a brief glimpse of John, but he hung out with a bunch of other kids his age so she ignored him.

After dinner, Katherine's mother approached them and quietly whispered to Mary that she could follow her to her room. Katherine walked with them up the stairs, but left them when they arrived at her mother's bedroom. The countess held the door open for Mary and she carefully stepped inside. Then the countess told her to sit in one of the rocking chairs opposite the bed. "What is it that you want to talk to me about?" the countess asked.

"Well, Ma'am," Mary paused.

"You do not have to address me so formally. It would be more comfortable for me if you didn't call me Ma'am or Countess of Warwick. Maybe you could call me Lady Beauchamp."

"Okay, Lady Beauchamp, I wanted to talk to you about your beautiful brooch. How long has this beautiful piece been in your family?"

"Why do you ask me this?"

"Well, it is a complicated story, but before we left on vacation my mother showed me one just like it."

"I don't see how that would be possible. This is the only one of its kind and my grandfather made it especially for my grandmother."

"Oh . . ." Mary paused. "I don't know what to say. The pin is gorgeous and very unique."

"Yes, it is. I cherish it and someday I will pass it on to my oldest daughter, Katherine when she gets married."

"She is a lucky girl," Mary said.

"Is there anything else you want to ask me?" the countess asked.

"Not really, I just wanted to meet you and have a chance to talk with you without so many people around. Our visit here at the castle has been very pleasant and I appreciate being able to stay here. Now, I should leave so that you can get your rest. Katherine is expecting me back soon. Thank you for talking with me." Mary stood and bowed to her great-grandmother and then turned and left the room.

Returning to her room she found Katherine still awake and looking through her backpack. Wanting to avoid all the questions about the things inside she decided to sidetrack Katherine by asking her lots of questions. "Have you ever heard a story about a big black dog with red eyes that dart all around the floor area?" Mary asked. "He roams the castle and some people even hear him growl."

"No, I have not." Katherine said.

"It's one of the stories that I've been told. I also heard that a little girl haunts the cellar or storage rooms here in the castle. Also servant ghosts go about their duties every night."

"How many stories have you heard?"

"I don't know how many. There's one where a ghost appears in a portrait in the study, and you can hear footsteps. And another one tells about apparitions seen walking within the tower walls. And there is a man by the name of Greville whose servant murdered him after an argument over money. The servant then turned the knife on himself. I think they told us on the ghost tour that it happened about 1628."

"Mary, that is not possible. It is only 1397."

Oh no, I've done it again. I have got to quit telling her about things that are in the future. Maybe that is why John and I can't find the place where the ghost tour was. It hasn't been built yet. "You are right Katherine, those things couldn't have happened."

"Where did you hear all of this stuff?" Katherine asked.

"On the Internet, when we looked for stuff to do while on vacation." *Whoops. What is wrong with me? Every time I open my mouth out pops something else I shouldn't be saying.* Mary didn't wait for Katherine to ask her any more questions she just said. "You know it's getting late. I think I need some sleep.

Then Mary thought of something else to say, "Where have the guys been all day?"

"I am not sure, but I think they went off with the men to talk about the war."

"Oh . . . that's what's been going on. Maybe before I lie down I better go find John for a minute."

Mary slipped quietly out of the room and went down the hall to Richard's room. She tapped lightly on the door and waited for someone to answer. When the door opened she couldn't see inside, but assumed she spoke to Richard and asked if she could talk to John. Next thing she knew John stood beside her in the hall. "What do you want?" he growled.

"What have you been doing all afternoon?"

"We've been planning what we are going to do the next time the castle is attacked. Why?"

"When are we going to find Mom and Dad?" Mary wiped her eyes and sniffled a bit.

"I'm not sure what we are going to do about that. I have spent the day trying to help the guys convince the Earl that he must not go alone to the banquet with the King, but he's leaving in the morning. Now I'll have time to help you find mom and dad," he looked at his sister's sad face. "I promise Mary, we'll find them soon."

Chapter Thirteen – The Crusade Begins

Several days later John and Richard watched as the guards stopped several men as they approached the castle. The men brought news that the Earl had been arrested and taken to the Tower of London.

"What kind of charges are there against him?" Richard asked.

"Treason."

"No!" yelled Richard. "We tried to tell dad that they only invited him to the go to the banquet so they could get him there without all his men."

"Gloucester and Arundel were also invited but they refused to go, but word is that they are both to be arrested. The King is insisting that the three men are all traitors," the messenger explained.

All the men in the castle, including John, spent the entire day behind closed doors planning a crusade. Mary could hardly wait to talk with John.

Just before bedtime Mary knocked on the boy's door. When John appeared she asked, "So what is happening?"

John briefly told her about the Earl being arrested.

"No!" Mary screamed. "They can't arrest my grandpa."

"Shhh, don't be so noisy. Someone might hear you."

"That's okay. I don't care."

"Well, I do. No one else is supposed to know about this. If they hear you they'll know I told."

Mary stood watching John's silhouette in the dark. He reached over and put his arm around her. "Things will soon be back to normal."

Mary shook her head, "I don't think things will ever be normal again. Are you going after him?"

"Yes."

"You won't go leaving me here alone will you?"

"I might have to," John said.

"No!" Mary screamed again.

John grabbed her by the shoulders and shook her. "You have to be quiet, or we'll both be in trouble."

"I'm sorry," she whimpered. "Please don't leave me behind. I don't want to be here without you. If you leave, take me with you. Promise."

John just stood in the hallway and didn't say anything.

Mary grabbed his arms and shook it. "Promise me you'll take me with you, John," she said.

"But Mary, its only men that are going I can't take you."

"Yes you can. You know that I can ride a horse as well as anyone."

"But you don't look like a man."

"I can fool anyone. I'll find something to wear and keep it on under my tunic all the time. It'll only take a second when you say we are ready to go."

"But . . . what about your hair? It's pretty long."

"If I wear it in a pony tail and put on a cap no one will know I'm a girl."

"But what if there is fighting?"

"If it gets too much I can hide."

John chuckled. "That's what I thought."

"You have to take me John. Now promise."

"Okay. I promise. I will not leave you alone. You probably can fool some of them and I'm positive you can ride a horse better than the best of them."

"Thanks John," Mary gave him a quick hug and slipped back down the hall to Katherine's room.

* * *

Almost before day light, John shook Mary awake. "Quick . . . come. We have to get a horse and be ready in just a few minutes. Here's a cap. I'll wait for you outside the door."

With that, he left the room. Before going to bed last night Mary had slipped her Levis on under her tunic. *Since the guys also wear tunics I hope this one is okay.* She pulled the cap over her ponytail and slipped out of the room. Mary and John quickly went to the barn.

They each picked a horse, put on the bridle, a blanket and saddle, mounted and waited for the others to come. Mary breathed a sigh of relief when no one talked to her or even asked about her. They both stayed as far away from Richard as they could. *If we can stay away from him until we are too far away to turn back, then I can go with them*, Mary thought.

The two tried to stay in large groups and neither of them said a word except to one another. They rode all day, and then about dark, the large group of men pulled over to the side and prepared to rest for the night. They didn't build a fire, so that meant that they would not have any warm food. After taking care of their horses, they helped themselves to some pieces of dried meat as well as dried fruit. John pulled Mary aside and took her to a stream for a drink of water. They avoided Richard and chose a place on the other side of camp from him to spread their blankets. Mary fell to sleep before her head even hit the ground.

The sun hadn't even come up when Mary heard the men stirring. She pulled John aside, "How far away are we going?" she whispered.

"They say that it's a three day ride."

Mary nodded her head, and walked over to the horse she had ridden yesterday. She got it ready to go, and then slipped into the saddle. She felt hungry, but didn't want to talk, so just waited hoping that someone would give her something to eat soon. After they had been in the saddle for a couple of hours, someone passed some hard biscuits around. "They are scones," John said.

Mary nodded her head again. She didn't dare talk or they would hear her high voice and her accent. If anyone heard her, she knew they'd never believe she was a boy. Once again they rode all day long and after dark they found a place to bed their horses and themselves. The next day started out the same as the two before. Mary felt sure they would never get to where they wanted to go. She didn't dare grumble because then John would say, "I told you so."

By now, John would sometimes talk to Richard, but Mary still kept her distance. She didn't want any more of Richard's attention because she didn't feel old enough to have some guy chasing after her. She also didn't want anyone to find out about her. Mary watched Richard and John laughing as they rode ahead of her. She brushed a tear away and followed behind with her head down.

Just before the sun went down, she noticed several large towers ahead. *I wonder if that's the Tower of London*, Mary thought. She slowed her horse and watched ahead. In front of her stood a huge square white tower with a tall wall that circled it. She pulled her horse to a stop and counted 13 small towers. As her eyes followed the wall from one end to the other she noticed at each corner round structures projecting outward from the main enclosure. On the other side of the tower a large river flowed past.

The large group of men became more enthusiastic the closer they got to their destination. Now it was hard to keep up with them as they rushed toward the towers, but Mary continued to follow. In front of them, she observed an archway, with towers on both side, and a latticed gate made of wood blocking the entrance. As they moved closer, she could see that they could raise or lower the gate with chains or ropes. In the middle of the causeway and prior to the gate was a drawbridge. The leader of the group raised his hand and everyone stopped.

"What is that square white tower?" someone asked.

"It's a complex of several buildings within two rings of defensive walls and a moat," the leader answered.

"What do you want?" a guard asked.

"We have come to see the Earl of Warwick Castle," the leader of the group answered.

"Before you can come inside you have to leave your horses outside and surrender your weapons. No one gets inside with any weapons."

Each man dismounted and tied their horses up and then walked past the guard, giving up a sword, gun, or knife. Those who refused had to stay behind. After that, the men were told that a guide would show them where they could go. First he led them toward the drawbridge. Mary gulped as she saw the huge moat filled with water under her as she slowly walked across the bridge. She felt frightened because she had no idea where John had gone. *Why does he always leave me alone?* She tried to be brave and continued forward.

Mary remembered reading online about these guards called Yeoman Warders at the Tower of London. They had been appointed bodyguards for King Henry VIII. She also knew they called them beefeaters. The Chief Warder dressed in a long red coat and Tudor bonnet led them. She looked around to see if his second-in-command was anywhere around. She hoped not because she knew that he would be carrying an axe.

Mary hoped that John was up there somewhere. She didn't want to be here without him, but she had no idea where he had disappeared to. Everything fascinated her but she decided she better concentrate on where she was going. *A person could get lost in here,* she thought. Because the guide knew the leader, Mary realized he explained to everyone what was going on.

"We just went past the Middle Tower. You will not be able to get past here tonight without a password. To the left is Mint Street. Notice the tavern with the golden chain sign. The tower we just walked through is called Byward. Behind this tower is the Bell Tower – it is the round building with the belfry on top. If you had come here to attack us, the bell would have been rung in alarm, and the drawbridge would have been raised and the gates shut."

Pointing with his staff the guide continued, "Ahead to the left, the square one is Bloody Tower, and Wakefield Tower is round. To the right is the back of St. Thomas's tower and Traitors' Gate. I am sure this is the gate they brought the Earl through because all important prisoners come this way."

They approached what they called the green and the guide stopped for a few minutes. He pointed out the White Tower and continued his narration. "This tower is 90 feet high and the walls are about 15 feet thick. This is where the King of England lives with his family. Also this is where the laws of the land are made. There is also a chapel inside. In the basement is an ancient old well built by the Romans." The guide paused and pointed, "To the west is where I am sure the Earl is being kept. Make sure you all stay here and wait until you are permitted inside."

Mary continued to look toward the green where many ravens dug around. She knew they were not a friendly bird and knew from experience that she shouldn't touch or feed them. She would like to chase them and scare them, but controlled her impulse. Mary remembered reading that the presence of these ravens protects the Crown and the tower; a superstition that if the Tower of London ravens are lost or fly away, the Crown will fall and Britain with it. *I wonder if they clip the raven's wings.*

Mary anxiously watched to see who they would choose to go inside. They chose Richard to be one of the first to go see his father. Mary didn't know the others that they allowed to go inside, but since they didn't choose John maybe now he would come and find her.

She stood off to the side waiting for him to locate her. She watched him looking around and then finally their eyes locked. John smiled and waved and Mary nodded her head.

"I sure hope we are still here at 10 o'clock, so we can see the Ceremony of Keys ceremony," John said.

"Me too," Mary whispered. "What shall we do now?"

John shrugged. "I don't know, but we better not go far. I wouldn't want to be left behind when they decide to let us inside."

By now, it was pitch dark except for the lanterns that hung around the different towers. "Too bad they don't have electricity," Mary said.

"Yeah, it is, although I really don't mind it like this. Maybe we have too many modern conveniences. I haven't minded the way we have had to live the past few days. I don't even think I miss my IPod that much."

"I doubt that," Mary said. "You never left it alone on the entire trip here."

John started to protest and then probably realized that Mary was right because he sure clamped his mouth shut quick. Mary watched the men around her. She hoped that no one knew her, but doubted that they did, because no one had confronted her. Even Richard had kept his distance. "John, has Richard suspected anything?" Mary asked.

"Nope."

"That's a big surprise."

"Not really, you really do make a pretty good guy."

Mary slugged him in the shoulder. "That isn't nice."

John smiled. "I know. I'm sorry."

The two moved back into the shadows and Mary asked, "Why have they arrested the Earl?"

"They say he is a traitor – to the king."

"I don't believe that," Mary said. "What did he do wrong?"

John shrugged. "I'm not real sure, but it has something to do with King Richard. He is accusing the Earl of Warwick with treason."

"Why?"

"I'm not sure. From what I've heard about King Richard he sounds like a young cocky kid to me. He became king when only ten. His uncle dominated the position. I read that King Richard made false promises all the time. His enemies placed limits on his power and later he took revenge on them. I'm sure this is one of those times."

"What else do you know about it?" Mary asked.

"They arrested him as a part of the Earl of Arundel's alleged conspiracy."

"What is that?"

"Please stop interrupting me. Let me finish the story and then you can ask questions." John paused for a few minutes, and then continued. "On the internet it says they imprisoned him in the Tower of London, and he pleaded guilty and threw himself on the mercy of the king. He had to forfeit his estates and titles, and they sentenced him to life imprisonment on the Isle of Man."

"Does that mean that Richard and Katherine have to move?" Mary asked.

John just looked at her. "I'm sorry," she said.

He nodded and continued. "I don't know if the family moved, we'll have to ask his children."

"But they won't know because he hasn't been sentenced yet."

"You're right. Can I tell the rest of the story now?"

Mary nodded and John continued. "The next year they moved him back to the Tower and then they released him in August 1399.

After pausing again John said, "I don't know how to answer your questions. My teacher at school told me that the politics in England are confusing. It seems that when King Richard took over the business of government himself, he sidelined many of the nobles, such as our great-grandpa. He turned to his inner circle of favorites for his council. The nobles he had snubbed didn't like it. In 1387, the English Parliament under pressure demanded that King Richard remove his unpopular councilors. When he refused, they told him that since he was still a minor, a Council of Government would rule in his place. After a battle, King Richard's men disposed of them and they forced him to accept new ones. He didn't have any authority."

Mary looked very confused. "Don't worry little sister, after King Henry IV took over, they restored great-grandpa to his titles and estates. Things are going to work out."

"Are you sure," Mary asked.

"Yes, Mary. We studied it in school, and I read it on the Internet, but I guess he'll have to stay here for awhile. At least until they prove his innocence."

"I wish I could have gotten to know him better. I did visit with his wife the other night in her room."

"Really," John said. "What's she like?"

"She's real nice and wouldn't even let me call her countess. She wanted me to call her Lady Beauchamp."

"What else did she say?" John asked.

"I asked to look at her brooch. That's about all that happened."

"I also talked to great-grandpa a few days ago for awhile," John said. I didn't know what to say, so I don't have much to tell. I know he is a great warrior and has been in many battles."

"Oh, you men. I don't know why you always want to talk about wars."

"It's just something that we like. Men like adventure."

"Yeah, adventure. Men like to get beat up. They like to be left along the side of the road bleeding to death. To me that is just plain stupid."

John laughed. "Girls are just wimps, always afraid of a little blood."

"No we aren't. It isn't the blood that is bad, it's the violence. Why do you always want to fight everyone?"

John shrugged. "I don't know. It's just something that we all do. I guess it is part of being a man. If we didn't do it people would call us sissies."

"What would be so bad about that?" Mary asked.

John shrugged again. "I don't know."

"You're repeating yourself."

"I guess it's just human nature. I'm a guy and you're . . ."

"Don't say that here," Mary said.

"Whoops. You're right. We better talk about something else before someone overhears us."

"Is your watch still working?" Mary asked.

"I don't know. I haven't even bothered to look at it."

John turned his arm over and tried to see the hands on the watch. "I think it's working, but I don't know if I changed it from Utah time or not. It says that it's eight-thirty."

"I think you might have changed it, because that seems like about the right time. I just didn't know if our batteries would work in this century. It seems that most everything else doesn't work."

Mary slipped back into the shadows as a couple of men approached. "Good to see you John. It looks like you had to bring your little brother with you," a heavy set man said.

"Yeah, either that or I had to stay behind."

"Too bad," another guy said as he slapped John on the shoulder.

"Oh, Mar . . . vin isn't so bad. He rides a horse as well as any of the guys."

"That's good," the man said as he looked toward Mary.

She kept her head down and didn't speak. "It looks like he's a bit shy."

"Yeah, he doesn't like strangers," John said.

A tall man walked over to John and said, "Since you're friends with the Duke's son do you think you'll be able to go inside?"

"I'm not sure, but I hope so."

They continued to talk for awhile, and Mary stayed hidden in the shadows of some trees. She thought the men would never leave and the longer they stayed the more nervous she became. She felt sure that with the slip of his tongue that John would soon blow her cover. At least, that's what he usually did. When the men finally moved on to talk to someone else she let out a sigh of relief. "Wow, they didn't leave any time too soon," she said.

"I'm sorry that they stayed so long," John said.

"It wasn't your fault. You weren't overly friendly so you didn't encourage them to stay."

"Maybe we need to see if we can find somewhere else to go," John said.

The two left the shadows of the trees and started to walk toward the tower where they held the Earl. John stopped for a minute under a torch and looked at his watch. "It's almost ten o'clock," he told Mary.

"Good. Now we can watch the Ceremony of the Keys. I hoped that we would still be here."

"Me too. Let's try to get a little ways away from all these men," John said.

"That's a great idea," Mary said as she hurried away. "Just don't get so far away that we can't watch the guards as they come by."

Mary found a comfortable spot on the ground next to the tower and leaned her head back to rest. She kept jerking her head because she had a hard time staying awake. Once in a while John would give her a nudge. Finally, he reached down to pull her to her feet. "Here they come."

Mary couldn't believe her eyes. She had always wanted to see their beautiful uniforms, but never dreamed their steps would be so precise. Their backs were ramrod straight and they never missed a beat. Her heart beat fast with pride as she watched the performance. From surfing the Internet she knew they did this same ceremony every single night. The Englishmen must be proud of their country.

Chapter Fourteen – Entering the Prison

After watching the key ceremony, Mary and John noticed that Richard had come out of the tower. "I'm going to go talk with Richard," John said.

Mary nodded her head and chose to stay put. After only a few minutes, John ran back to her. "We have to go now," he said breathing hard. "They are only letting a few of us in."

"How come I get to go with you? Did you tell him about me?"

"No, I wouldn't do that. I just told him I had a friend who wanted to go inside."

The two got in a line with several other men and then they opened the door for them to enter. Mary couldn't believe that they let almost the entire group go inside. She tried hard to stay next to John, but since she was so small she soon found herself pushed ahead. Mary had no way of knowing where John had gone because everyone stood taller than her. She just went along with the crowd. After all, she didn't have much choice. They were all much bigger and stronger than her.

Soon she found herself below some steps and the men started pushing forward. Mary had no choice but to go up the stairs or be trampled. At the top she finally got out from between so many men. She felt her cap being pulled off, but held it firmly in place. She moved to the side of everyone right up against the stone wall. Everyone seemed to be pushing at once and her feet got sore from so many men stepping on her.

It took all her will power to keep from screaming, but if she did that, her secret would be out. She bit her tongue and took several deep breathes. Mary had to get control so she could somehow get out of here and find John. She pushed flat against the wall and scooted further back away from everyone. Mary could hear shouting and questions and so much noise. She wanted so much to go back downstairs, but could find no path to the stairs. Too many bodies were in front of her. *These men are sure rude,* Mary thought. *They don't care about anyone.*

She heard some of the men grumbling about how the Earl would not let them help him. "He said that he was grateful that we wanted to help, but he would feel responsible if anyone was hurt and that we should all wait for another time. He says he is innocent so there should be no problem."

"You mean he is going to wait for his trial?" a man nearby asked.

The first man nodded.

"He is a fool. They are not going to let him go," another man shouted.

Mary had difficulty breathing because so many people stood in the tiny upstairs room. The smell of their bodies made her sick to her stomach. She knew if she didn't get out soon she would throw-up. She was tired of all this talk so she pushed herself toward where she thought the stairs would be. Surprisingly some of the men stepped aside to let her past. Although several men still stood on the steps because there was no more room upstairs they let her past. At the bottom she found John. "You look sick," he said.

She only nodded her head and continued past him. He turned to follow her. "Did you get to see him?" John asked.

Mary shook her head, but didn't talk. She had to take several deep breaths before she dared to even whisper. "No, there were too many men up there."

"Why did you go upstairs?" John asked.

"I had no choice, they pushed me up there," Mary whispered.

John nodded his head in understanding.

"It smelled worse than a wet dog up there with all those sweaty bodies," Mary said.

John wanted to laugh but knew he better not, or he would get a hard smack from Mary. Instead he helped her get to the outside door so she could breathe in some fresh air. While the two stood in the doorway Mary whispered, "The Earl won't let us rescue him."

"You're kidding," John shouted.

"Shhhh. Everyone is looking at you," Mary said.

"Sorry. But why did we come here if he won't let us help?" John asked.

Mary shrugged her shoulders and the two stepped outside so that some of the men could leave. When it looked like most of them had gone the two kids went back inside. The downstairs room was empty except for a few men. Many men still crowded the stairs so they continued to wait. More men came down the steep narrow stairs and John and Mary finally went up. They still couldn't get anywhere close to the Earl, but at least only a few men stood in the way. Mary hung back and John tried to pull her forward. She shook her head, "No, I'll stay here," she whispered.

Understanding her meaning John let go of her arm and moved forward. Mary watched him approach the Earl, and bend to talk with him. She wished she could also talk with him, but if she did he would know she wasn't a guy because of her high voice.

After awhile she went back down the stairs, sure that John would soon follow. Her curiosity got the best of her and she went exploring down in the cellar. Other than a few spiders which frightened her, she didn't notice anything scary. She looked inside lots of barrels and wooden crates. Her feet hurt so she sat on one of the short wooden boxes and soon fell asleep.

After several hours, Mary awoke with a start. *Where am I?* Everything had turned black. Then she remembered her backpack and pulled it in front of her and felt for the zipper. Inside she found her flashlight. As soon as she noticed the box and glanced around the area, she remembered that she had gone to the cellar in the tower where they had the Earl in prison. Mary crept up the steps and couldn't find anyone. She went up to the top floor and saw the Earl lying on the hard floor asleep. She went back down the stairs and tried the door, but knew that it would be locked. *I wonder where John is, and how I'm going to get out of here.*

She sat on the floor next to the door and waited. She wished she had John's watch. At least she'd know how long she'd have to wait. Mary must have dozed because the next thing she knew someone unlocked the door next to where she sat. She stood behind the door, and hoped that she could slip out before anyone saw her. When the door came open it almost smashed her in the nose, but she crunched up tight against the wall. The person who came in just left the door open and headed upstairs. That gave Mary the perfect opportunity to sneak outside.

Of course, her troubles weren't over just because she had escaped from the prison. She still was locked inside a large compound with lots of towers and it might not be easy to get past the guards at the front gate. First, she had to remember how to get out of this big maze.

I sure hope that John didn't leave me.

Mary found herself wandering up and down first one path and then another one. She had no idea how she had got to where she was. By now, all the towers looked the same; some round and others square. Some made of stone and others made of wood. She heard soldier's behind her and quickly stepped aside. *Maybe I can follow them,* she thought.

Her next problem was going to be finding a way past the guard. Mary came to a hole in the wall and there stood a guard. He stood at attention, but she could tell he wouldn't let her outside without lots of questions. She lowered her voice and asked, *"How do I get out of here?"*

"How did you get in?" he asked.

"A guard let us in last night, but now everyone has left me."

"You have to have permission before I can let you past. How do I know that you aren't a prisoner trying to escape?"

"Do I look like a prisoner?" she asked. "Now tell me who gives permission?"

"Someone in authority," he answered.

"Who lives here?"

"Other than the royal family, there are only high status prisoners here."

Mary looked up a hill north-west of the tower. She was sure it was called Tower Hill, but she wasn't going to ask any more questions. "Well, I'll see you later," she said and turned and ran as fast as she could across the draw bridge.

"Wait," the guard called after her.

"No, I can't; I need to get back home."

She knew he couldn't come after her, or he would have to leave his post. She was sure that wasn't allowed so she was sure she'd be safe for now. Still, she had no idea where John was. *What am I going to do? I wonder how to get back to the Castle.*

Once outside the gate Mary didn't see very many horses. Those she saw could belong to almost anyone. Up the hill in the distance, she could see lots of horses moving away from her. *Why did they take my horse? Why wouldn't John wait for me? There is no way that I can run fast enough to catch them. Now what am I going to do? It took three days to get here by horse. I could never walk that far.*

Mary decided she better get going but as the day grew longer, she dragged her feet and walked slower and slower. She got tired and looked for a place to rest under a tree. Mary was so exhausted that soon her eyelids drooped and she fell fast asleep.

Suddenly she awoke. *Where is John?* She wondered. She jumped up and looked around, and then she remembered. She knew she was far behind and she had no idea where John had gone. *What am I going to do?* she cried. *How am I ever going to make it to the castle without a horse? Where am I? That's a good thing there isn't anyone else on the path. How would I explain myself? What would I tell them if they asked any questions?*

Mary kept to the edge of the path and watched for any movement in front or behind her. She didn't want to run across anyone. *I wonder if I'm even going the right way. I just know this is the way the horses are headed. It has to be the way John is going. How did I lose track of him? I bet he'll be angry when I find him. If I find him.*

She caught the tears as they slid down her face. *Now stop that Mary. You can't let John catch you crying.* She stomped her foot. *How's he going to catch me crying if I can't even find him?*

The path led her farther and farther into the country. Mary wasn't sure if this was the way to the Warwick Castle. *How many days did it take us to get here?* Mary started counting on her fingers. *One, two, three, or was it four days?* Mary couldn't remember. *Why did John let me come? He should have talked me out of this.*

She couldn't answer her own questions. *He knows that I hate wars, so why would I willingly come with him in search of action. There's no way that I want to see where the knights are fighting. Why would a war be going on for a hundred years? No one would want to fight that long. No one would live that long. They must certainly be crazy.*

Once Mary decided she didn't want to be involved in a war she made up her mind that she was somehow going to find John, or at least find her way back to the Warwick Castle. *Mom and Dad have to be there. That's where John and I left them. All we did was buy two tickets to go on a haunted walk. It wasn't even supposed to last an hour, not for weeks.*

Mary kept walking and walking. There was no one around, and no signs posted anywhere. *What if I'm going the wrong way?* Then Mary did the only thing she could think of doing. She fell to her knees and pleaded with the Lord to help her. *Please Father in Heaven, help me. I have no idea what to do. Help me to know the right direction to get back to the Warwick Castle. Help me find a way to find my mom and dad. Thank you. In the name . . .*

After her prayer was finished, she continued to kneel. She remembered her teacher at church telling them that they needed to sit still and listen for an answer to their prayers. As she knelt in the dirt she heard a voice calling to her, "Mary, Mary, where are you?"

Mary looked up and then turned around. She couldn't believe her eyes. Two men rode toward her. She stood and shaded her eyes so that she could see more clearly. It was John and Richard. "Where have you been?" John shouted.

"What do you mean where have I been, where have you been?" Mary put her hands on her hips and glared at John.

"We've been looking for you. The rest of the men left early, but we kept looking for you."

Mary ducked her head, "I thought you left me."

"Why would I do that?"

"I don't know. I got locked inside the prison over night and when I woke up you had left me."

"I didn't know you stayed in the prison. I finally told Richard about you coming with me. We spent the entire night looking for you. By morning we panicked, but told the others to go on without us because we had to stay and find you."

"I cannot believe that you thought a girl could come with a bunch of men," Richard said. "You really had me fooled. Most girls have no idea how to handle a horse as well as you do."

Mary smiled at the two of them. "I'm really sorry. I didn't know what to do. When I finally ran over the drawbridge, I could see a bunch of horses far ahead. I just thought you had left me."

"No way, Sis, I would never do that. Mom and Dad would skin me alive if I left you to fend for yourself."

"How did you get past that guard at the gate?" Richard asked.

"It wasn't easy. I just finally ran as fast as I could. I knew he couldn't follow me without leaving his post, and it's not like he has a phone or anything."

"What?" Richard asked.

Oh no, I've done it again, Mary said to herself.

"That was really cleaver of you," John said, "And really brave."

Mary was grateful that John was trying to distract Richard and get him talking about something else. She was always opening her big mouth. She wondered if she would ever learn to think before she spoke.

"What are we going to do now?" Mary asked.

"I think we should be heading home," Richard said. "I am glad that we brought your horse with us although it was tempting to leave it for you in case you showed up."

"I'm glad you brought it too, because I had no idea which horse was mine. I saw a few horses by the gate, but I didn't even think that one of them was the one I had ridden here."

"It's a good thing we decided to bring it because it's too far back to go and get it," John said.

Mary climbed up on the horse, and started following the two guys. "Richard, I still don't understand why we are leaving without your father."

"Neither do I," Richard answered. "His men spent hours last night trying to reason with him, but he kept saying over and over, 'I am innocent. I do not want anyone hurt trying to help me.'"

Mary nodded her head. *I'm sure glad that my grandfather doesn't want war any more than I do.* Then she asked, "When are we going to eat?"

John laughed. "That's all you ever think about."

"No it's not, but it's been a long time since I had any real food."

Richard assured her that as soon as they found some shade to protect them from the sun they would rest the horses and share some food with her. That satisfied Mary and she kept pinching herself wondering if all of this was for real. It had certainly been a bad dream. This time Mary didn't try to get away from Richard. She was glad that the two had found her because she was certainly tired of walking. As the threesome rode side by side John asked, "How did you manage to get locked in the prison?"

"Well, while I was waiting for you to come downstairs I inspected the cellar. I just sat down for a minute, and I guess I fell fast asleep. The next thing I knew it was so dark I couldn't even see my hands in front of my face. It's a good thing I had my trusty flashlight."

"What is a flashlight?" Richard asked.

"It's something that Mary has that lights up when she turns it on. I'm sure you've never seen one before," John said.

"Well, I would like to see it," Richard said.

"When we stop to eat I'll show it to you," Mary said. "I'll do almost anything for food."

John laughed so hard Mary thought he was going to fall off his horse. "You got that right, Sis, I believe you would do anything for a meal."

"I'll race you to those trees up ahead," Mary said.

Richard actually beat everyone there, but the other two were close behind. They sat in a circle, and Richard opened his saddlebag and pulled out some food. Mary had no idea what she was eating, except the fact that it was food and she was starved. After the quick meal, Mary pulled off her backpack and zipped it open. Richard reached for it, and played with the zipper awhile before reaching inside. "I have never seen anything like this."

"No, I'm sure you haven't," John said. "You'll also be surprised with most of the stuff that you'll find inside."

First Richard pulled out Mary's jacket. He tossed it aside, as well as the t-shirt. Then he reached deep inside and pulled out a rectangular pink thing. Richard had a questionable look on his face. "That's a phone," Mary said.

"What is it used for," Richard asked.

"To call people."

Richard shrugged then reached inside the bag again and pulled out the bright red flashlight. John reached over, and took it from him and turned the dim light on. At first Richard didn't understand until John pulled his hand over to where the light was shining. "In the dark it makes it so you can see where you are going."

Richard nodded his head, "I see."

"Before I forget we better find the batteries for the flashlight. I would hate to be in trouble when it gets dark. Can you see them in there?"

"What do they look like?"

Mary removed the old batteries from the flashlight and Richard hunted through the bag until he saw what she needed. "I need two of them," Mary said.

Once she put the batteries in place Richard continued his search through the bag. He reached in and pulled out several ponytail holders, a brush, lip-gloss, notebooks, paper and pens. Inside he could still feel several books. "You really do carry a lot of things with you."

Mary nodded her head. "You never know when you are going to need something."

"Show me the phone," Richard said.

"It won't do any good," John said. "It doesn't work here in England."

"Where does it work?"

"At home," Mary answered.

"Tell me where this Utah is," Richard asked.

"Across the ocean," John said.

"How did you get here?" Richard asked.

"On an airplane," John answered.

Now it's John's turn to say something stupid. At least it's not me this time. Mary smiled anticipating Richard's reaction. She continued smiling while John tried to get himself out of this predicament. At least now, John was doing the explaining. If she had said anything about an airplane, John would be waiting to get on her case about it.

Soon the three knew that it was time for them to mount up and be on their way. The horses had rested enough and although Mary was sure it would take her days before she was well rested she was anxious to be back to the castle. She still wasn't sure how she and John were ever going to find their parents, but at least they would be back to where they had been when they had gone back in time.

Chapter Fifteen – Returning to the Castle

Along the way, the three conversed comfortably. Mary found herself liking Richard, but not in the way she worried about, but as a dear friend. Although his ways were different from hers, she thought he could be put in the class of a 'cool guy'.

Night came and then morning again. She guessed that they had another day before they would be home. *Home? What am I thinking? This isn't home.* But to Mary it really did feel like home. These people felt like family.

She hadn't had much of a chance to get to know the Earl, and now with him in prison she knew she never would become acquainted with him. But his wife, the countess, felt like a real grandma. Mary wondered if she would ever be able to tell her about their relationship. Back in 1812 she and John had been able to tell Grandpa Holt who they really were. He felt okay with that. Now she wondered if she and John could ever tell Richard and Katherine who they were and where they really came from. She certainly hoped they would be able to disclose their identity.

They stopped to rest the horses and eat about midday. While Richard got the saddlebags John said, "I'm going to talk to Richard about time travel."

"Are you sure?" Mary asked.

"Yes. Maybe he'll have an idea how to get us back home."

"Okay. It certainly won't hurt any. He already thinks I'm crazy."

John laughed. "No, he doesn't"

While the three ate John cleared his throat. "Richard, there is something that Mary and I need to tell you."

"I am listening."

"Well, this is sort of complicated, and maybe you won't believe us, but Mary and I don't belong here."

"What do you mean that you do not belong here?" Richard asked.

"What he is trying to tell you is, that we live a long ways away," Mary said.

"I already know that," Richard said.

"Not just in miles, but also in time," John explained.

Richard didn't say anything he just looked at John and then at Mary. Then he sat there staring straight ahead.

"You aren't doing this very well, John," Mary said.

"I'd like to see you do it any better."

"I will. Richard, John and I are here from the future." Mary put her hands on her hips and said,
"How's that?"

Richard started to laugh. "You are both funny. I have never heard of anything this silly in my entire life."

"Really Richard. It's true," John said. "We are here on a vacation with our parents. Mary and I went on a Ghost Alive Tour at the Warwick Castle. During the tour, Mary stumbled and we fell into a wall that opened up. We couldn't get back through the wall, but we found another secret passageway and ended up in your library. We can't find our way back to our parents."

Mary interrupted, "We thought if we told you about it that maybe you could help us find our way home. Here in the 14th century we have no home because the pilgrims haven't even crossed the ocean yet. Until they discover America we aren't even alive."

No one spoke for several minutes and then John plunged in again. "The valley in Utah didn't even start until after the pioneers went west in 1847."

Richard looked puzzled, and shook his head. "Is that why you talk so funny?" he asked.

"Yes, that's it," Mary said.

"This is really hard to believe," Richard said. "But no one I know could ever make up a story like this. You are telling me the truth, right?"

Both Mary and John nodded. "We wouldn't lie to you," John said.

"No, our parents taught us to not lie. You are our friend and friends tell the truth to each other," Mary said.

Richard sighed. "Can we talk about this later? I am tired, and we need to find a place to rest for the night. I hope that we can get home by tomorrow."

"Yes, we can talk about it tomorrow," John said.

* * *

After mounting their horses the following morning Richard immediately asked, "So you found a secret door in the library?"

"Yeah, we did," Mary said.

"Does everyone talk like you two?" Richard asked.

"All the young people do," John said.

"There is so many words that the two of you use that I have no idea what they mean. And your accent is really weird," Richard said.

"What words don't you understand?" John asked.

"For instance Mary said, "Yeah". What does that mean?"

"It means yes," Mary answered.

"Maybe you should just stop us each time that we say something that you don't understand," John suggested.

"If I did that, I would stop you after almost every word," Richard said.

"What word didn't you understand in the last sentence," John asked.

"Last time you said didn't and the time before you said don't. We Englishmen never use those words," Richard explained.

John smiled. "I guess we do use a lot of slang. Didn't means did not and don't means do not. We just shorten the word and instead of saying two words we just say one."

"Now can we get back to talking about Richard helping us find our mom and dad?" Mary asked.

"How did you find the hidden wall?" Richard asked.

"Well, Mary shined her flashlight ahead and I kept banging on all the new walls that we saw. When I found one that sounded different we investigated it."

Richard nodded. "Go on."

"We both pushed on the area around the hollow sound and it started to move."

Mary interrupted, "We soon fell into a room full of books. The best sight I had seen for hours. Those guards in the dungeon are really scary."

"You went down to the dungeon?" Richard asked.

"Well, not on purpose, but yeah we did," Mary admitted.

Richard shook his head. "I would never go down there, not ever. There are three entrances, but I avoid them."

"It'll be at least a million years before I ever do that again," Mary agreed.

"Good, because there are only real bad people down there, and I would not want to have you getting hurt," Richard said.

"Where are the other entrances?" John asked.

"There is a trap door under the staircase outside the great hall, and I think there is an outside entrance," Richard answered.

"Why would there be one outside?" John asked.

"The only reason I can think is so that the bad men do not have to come into the castle. John, maybe you both need to start the story from the beginning. That way there will not be any surprises and I might know better how to help you."

"Okay." Mary said. "Do you want to start first John?"

"No, you go ahead."

"I really liked the scary ghost tour."

"No, you didn't," John interrupted.

Mary ignored him and continued with the story. Then she took a breath and John started telling the story. "I have read some books telling about an opening in the wall that led to undisclosed tunnels. They said that old castles in England had ways that the knights could escape without anyone seeing them. So, I convinced Mary that's what we had to do to find one. I started tapping the wall with my pocketknife, first up one side and then down the other."

"A pocketknife?" Richard asked.

"Yeah, want to see it," John reached into his pocket and pulled out a small metal object and handed it over to Richard.

Richard turned it over and looked at it carefully. John pulled his horse next to Richard and reached over and opened one of the blades. Richard gasped. "Oh, I have never seen anything like this. How do you get the blade out?"

John put the blade in and then once again opened it.

"That is nice. I wish I had one," Richard said.

"Then keep it," John said.

"No. I could not do that," Richard said.

"Why not? It belongs to me and you are my friend and if I want to give it to you I can. Besides when I get home I can buy myself another one."

"Really?" Richard asked.

John nodded. "Yeah, all the guys have them and even some girls. They don't cost much and I can get another one really easy like."

"Now on with the story," Mary said. "The guard in the dungeon looked real mean."

"How did you get away from him?" Richard asked.

John laughed. "Mary stomped on his foot and we ran."

Now Richard took a turn at laughing. "In my younger years I did hear stories about hidden walls in the castle. The reason is exactly what you said, John. The knights or someone could escape and go get help from another castle. I never found a secret passageway, but as soon as we get to the castle we can investigate. Maybe Katherine could help us."

"With you and Katherine helping us, we can probably go to rooms that Mary and I couldn't go to alone," John said.

"Yeah, our parents wouldn't want us snooping around someone's house, but if you're with us that won't matter," Mary said. "How much longer before we get to the castle?"

"We are getting real close," Richard answered. "Mary, what are you going to tell Katherine when she asks where you have been for a week?"

Mary shrugged, "I don't know. I didn't really think anyone would miss me, but I guess Katherine would have wondered. I left without a word."

"You better just tell her the truth, Mary. Mom and Dad don't like us to lie. Besides we are going to be telling her about the time travel thing so she may as well know that you tried to fool everyone and rode off with all the men," John said while looking at his watch. "I bet we're going to be in time for dinner."

"Now it's you thinking about food," Mary said.

"What is that on your arm?" Richard asked.

"Oh, this is a watch," John answered. "It tells me what time it is."

"I have never seen such a thing," Richard said.

"I'm sure you haven't. I'd give it to you, but it wouldn't last you long because eventually the batteries would run low and since you don't have any here the watch wouldn't work any longer."

"You do not need to give me any more gifts. The pocketknife is enough. Seeing all the things you and Mary have makes me wish that I could go forward in time to your century."

"That would be hard for you," Mary said. "I think it is better to go back because you already know about those things, even though you miss some of the conveniences, but if you went forward everything would be totally different. You wouldn't know what to do."

"What kinds of things are so different?" Richard asked while looking at John.

"Well, if we had gone to London, we would have ridden in a car," John said. "It would have only taken us a few hours to get home."

Richard pulled his horse to a stop. "What are you telling me?" he asked. "No one can travel that fast."

"Yes, they can. They can even go faster than that. We flew over here to England on an airplane. If you can get a good connecting flight you can make the entire four-thousand-mile trip in about thirteen or fourteen hours."

Richard shook his head. "That is not possible."

"That's what I was trying to tell you," Mary said. "If you went forward in time, it would totally blow you away."

Richard turned and stared at her. "I have no idea what that means, but it sounds like I would be in for a real surprise if I came to live with you."

Mary nodded. "Yes, you would."

"The castle is just at the top of the hill. I will race you," Richard called to Mary.

The three arrived at the drawbridge at almost the same time. All of them were glad to be home, and all of them were out of breath. They walked the horses the rest of the way to the barn, and dismounting, unsaddled the horses, and made sure the horses had plenty of food to eat and ample water to drink before they went inside the castle.

Chapter Sixteen – Confession

Once inside they ran up the steps and Mary hurried to Katherine's room. She could hardly wait to wash and clean up for dinner. Never had she been so anxious for a good meal and she had so much to tell her dear friend, Katherine.

Mary hurried and washed her face and changed into another tunic. She hoped that Katherine would be in the room, but she must have already gone to the great hall. Of course, she wouldn't know that Mary had come back so there would be no reason for her to be waiting for her. She left the room and knocked on the door for Richard and John to join her. They pulled open the door and the three of them went below. They had no trouble finding Katherine and the dinner tasted great. Mary had a hard time containing her excitement and kept trying to get Katherine to hurry. After the meal, the four of them went outside for privacy so they could talk.

"We have something we want to talk with you about," Mary said looking directly at Katherine.

"Well, I have something I want to talk with you about too," Katherine said. "Where have you been? My mother and I have been worried about you."

Mary ducked her head. "Sorry, Katherine. I went with Richard and John to London."

"Why?" Katherine asked.

"I wanted to see what they had done with your father," Mary answered.

"And what have they done with my father?"

"Nothing. They have him in a prison," Richard said.

"Why?"

"They say he is a traitor, but he says he is not and would not let us help him escape."

"How long will he be there?' Katherine asked.

"We do not know. He told me to come home and he would send word about the upcoming trial," Richard explained.

Katherine shook her head and turned toward Mary. "But, I do not understand why you did not tell me you were leaving?"

"I thought that you would try to stop me."

"Yes, I would have. That is not something that we women do. You should not have gone," Katherine said.

Turning to Richard she asked, "Why did you let her go? Mamma is going to be upset with you."

"I did not know. She dressed like a boy and stayed away from me. I never saw her until we were on the way home from the London Towers."

"How long did it take you to get there?" Katherine asked.

"Three days," Mary said.

"There is no way that you should not have known Mary went with you," Katherine said as she poked Richard in the chest. "That is a long time."

Holding his arms up Richard said, "Really I did not know she had come with us until we were at the prison. Maybe John would never have told me if Mary had not got lost."

"You got lost?" Katherine asked as she turned toward Mary. "How?"

"I wasn't lost. I just fell asleep in the prison and they locked me in. I thought everyone had left to come back to the castle so I found my own way out and headed here."

Katherine shook her head. "That is an unbelievable story."

"If you think that is unbelievable wait until you hear the rest of the story. You will really be surprised," Richard said. "Maybe I should tell you some of it first."

Katherine nodded her head. "Go on, then."

"Well our friends here are from another place."

"I know that," Katherine said.

"No, you do not understand. They are not from the fourteenth century. They live in the future."

Katherine didn't speak, she only watched Richard close.

"That is why they talk so different, and they also dress strange and act peculiar. They are nothing like the people from our time."

"Have you been in the sun too long?" Katherine asked. "This that you are telling me is not possible."

"But, I promise you Katherine, it is all true. They need our help so please listen to their story," Richard begged.

Katherine looked at Mary and John and finally nodded her head. "Go ahead, I will listen."

John repeated to Katherine what he had told Richard and then asked, "Do you think you could help us find any more secret passageways?"

By now, Katherine smiled. "My younger sisters and I have found a few. Come and I will show them to you."

"What?" Richard asked. "You have never told me about this."

"No, we did not. We made a pact to keep it between ourselves. Besides you boys always stayed outside and did manly things. We did not think you would want to be bothered with such things."

"Won't your sisters be angry if you show us?" Mary asked.

"No, I think Margaret does not like this sort of thing anymore and I doubt that Elizabeth even remembers it because it took place a long time ago while she was still young."

She took Mary by the hand and pulled her toward the castle. Once inside they went to the library. "We already found one in here," Mary said.

"Really? Did you find the one in the next room?" Katherine asked as she turned toward the other room. "It is real small, and I would be surprised if you found that one."

As they entered the room, Mary stopped and stared. In the corner sitting on a desk sat a beautiful instrument that looked similar to her violin. "What a beautiful instrument. What is it called?"

"It is a rebec?" Katherine answered.

"Could I try it?" Mary asked.

"Yes. That would be fine."

Mary sat on a chair, and put the rebec under her chin and raised the bow to the strings.

"That is not the way you hold it," Katherine smiled.

"Oh, it looks similar to my violin so I thought you would play it the same way," Mary said. "What do I need to do?"

"Here, let me show you," Katherine suggested as she sat and held the instrument half way between her chin and waist.

After Katherine showed Mary what to do she handed the beautiful instrument over and Mary started to play the only song she really knew by heart, *America.* Although it only had 3 strings Mary was still able to struggle through the song before returning the instrument to its original place and sitting in a comfortable chair.

"That is a beautiful song," Katherine said. "Where did you learn it?"

"At school, and then from my violin teacher," Mary blushed and in a few minutes looked up from where she sat and noticed a portrait. "It's your mom and dad."

"Yes, it is," Katherine said. "Mother does not like it, but I think it looks like them. My father hated posing for it."

"You mean it is painted?" Mary asked.

"Yes. How else would you get a picture?"

"Never mind, it's too complicated. Now when are you going to show us the secret door?"

"Oh. It is right over here," Katherine said leading the way to the other side of the room.

"Where is it?" Richard asked.

Mary had almost forgotten that Richard and John had come with them because they hadn't said anything for a long time. The two boys had made their selves comfortable on the sofa nearby but now they followed the girls. It took Katherine a few minutes to find the exact spot, but soon the wall moved in and around and they found themselves in another room. Mary spook first. "Oh. This isn't the tunnel, it's another room."

Mary twirled around and around looking at everything. "This is the library, where John and I came from the tunnel."

"Why would there be a passageway from one room to another one?" John asked.

"I never knew this door was even here," Richard said. "I do not know why you would want to go from one room to another one."

"I guess if you were trapped in one room and knew you could go into another room to escape it would work," Mary said turning toward the inside wall. "Help me find the way into the tunnel."

The four hurried to the inside wall and John knocked around with his knuckles. "Do you remember exactly where it was?"

"No, I think I couldn't believe it when we fell through the wall, and so I didn't really pay any attention."

"You girls stand back and let Richard and I find it," John instructed.

Mary stood back, but she didn't want to. She knew she could hear every bit as well as John, but she didn't want to make a scene in front of their friends. She would let him be the big shot if that's what he wanted.

"I do not hear anything different," Richard said.

"You will. Let's go a little slower," John told Richard as he started back the other direction. "Wait. Listen now."

"Oh. That does sound a little different, but the wall looks the same to me. There are not any seams or indication that there is a door here," Richard said as he examined the wall on both sides of where John pointed.

"Yeah, it does look a little unusual right here," John slid his finger up and down the wall right in front of where the two boys stood. "We need to push, but we also need to be careful that we don't get in the way of the wall as it turns. I don't want us to go flying the way Mary and I did when we came here," John laughed.

Mary and Katherine stood still watching the two guys. Katherine looked surprised and watched with fascination. "We girls never found this place," she told Mary.

"You probably won't like it because it takes us into a dark tunnel," Mary said.

"How will we see where we are going?" Katherine asked.

"That won't be a problem. Remember I always carry my backpack. In fact, maybe I should get the light out ready for us," Mary said pulling the bag from her back and unzipping it to retrieve the flashlight.

"I wish I had one of those," Katherine said.

"When we find a way home, I'll give it to you to keep. It probably won't do you much good for long because the batteries will eventually run out. I do have some spare ones that I can leave with you, but when they are gone it won't be much use to you."

"That would be so nice, but I do not want to take your only light."

"You don't understand. I can buy myself another one. They don't cost much, and besides I want to leave something with you to help you remember me."

"There is no way that I will ever forget you," Katherine said.

"Nor I you. I don't have any friends back home like you."

"Hey, are you girls coming with us?" John asked.

"Yeah, sure we are," Mary said grabbing Katherine by the arm and pulling her toward the opening.

Mary turned on the light, and handed it to Katherine. "You keep track of it. Just shine it ahead so that everyone can see."

Katherine gasped as they entered the tunnel. "It is dark and a bit scary here."

John reached back to close the door but Mary cried out. "No. Don't close it. Leave it alone so we can get back inside."

"Oh, you are probably right. But what if someone sees it?"

"That will not matter," Richard said. "There is not anyone in the house that would be a threat to us."

John nodded his head. "Okay, we'll leave it open."

The foursome walked carefully up the path leading toward where Mary and John had first entered the tunnel. Every time they came to a turn, the two boys stopped to feel the walls. Mary and Katherine waited patiently for them to inspect everything that looked as though it might be a hidden doorway.

"I have not had this much fun in years," Katherine said.

"We neither," Mary declared. "Even when John and I went back in time to the War of 1812, I don't remember having this much fun."

"Is that something you do often?" Katherine asked.

"What?" Mary asked.

"You know, go back in time."

Mary shook her head. "No, just that one time," she laughed. "Well, also this time. It's not something that we plan on doing."

"How does it happen?" Katherine asked.

"I don't really know. This time we just went on a ghost tour and wham the next thing I knew we landed in this tunnel."

"I am glad you came," Katherine said.

"So am I," Mary said. "Except I miss my mom and dad, but I'm glad that I have a new friend. None of my friends back home are much fun. All they want to do is talk about boys. They act so silly."

The girls continued talking and hardly noticed what the boys were doing. A couple of times they thought they had found a secret passageway, but it didn't turn out to be so. At the end of the tunnel they all stopped. "So where is the doorway?" Mary asked.

John shrugged his shoulders, "I don't know. We must have missed it."

"Let us head back down and try again. Do you have any idea which side we should be looking on?" Richard asked.

"I really don't know," John said.

"Well, I do. It's on this side," Mary pointed to the stone wall in front of her.

"How do you know?" John asked.

"I remember because you reached down and pulled me up by my right hand. If you had pulled me up with the other one the wall would have been in the way."

Mary started feeling along the hard stonewall. "Were we at the end of the tunnel then?"

"I don't really know," John said. "I don't remember looking behind me. I just figured we needed to go down because when we headed to the ghost walk we climbed a hill."

"Yeah, I didn't look back either."

"How do we know where to start looking for the door?" Richard asked.

Both Mary and John shrugged their shoulders. "Katherine and I are going to help you this time," Mary said. "Katherine, hold the light closer to the wall, and I'll feel all along it as we head back to the library."

"Are you sure it is this direction from the library?" Richard asked.

"No, I'm not sure," Mary said.

"I'm not sure either," John answered. "I just assumed it would be this direction, but it could have been the other way."

This time they all paid closer attention to the indentations in the stone and everything that looked even a little bit different. They walked and walked. They found no indication that a secret door could be anywhere. "We have sure been doing this a long time," Richard said.

"Yeah, it has taken us a lot longer this time," John agreed.

"With four of us looking, I'm sure we haven't missed anything," Mary said.

Suddenly another path turned to the left. Mary stopped. "What happened to the library doorway?"

"I don't know," John said. "But we've gone past it because if we keep going straight we are going to end up in the dungeon."

"Are you sure?" Richard asked.

"I'm not going down there," Mary protested.

"It's okay Mary we aren't going to the dungeon," John said. "To answer Richard's question, yes we are sure. If you turn left there are guards walking back and forth. Mary and I were afraid of being captured so we decided to find our way back inside by way of another hidden door."

"There is no reason to be afraid of the guards," Katherine said. "Richard and I both know them, and they really will not hurt us."

"But what about the library?" Mary asked.

"Once outside, we can just go back inside through the outside door. That way we will not have to worry about finding the hidden door," Richard said.

"But I thought we should go find the other door so that John and I can go home," Mary complained. "Besides, who closed the door in the library?"

"We probably just missed it. No one would hurt us here. We will look for the door another day. I think we are all tired," Katherine said.

Richard and Katherine led the way outside and waved to the guards as though they knew them. John and Mary followed close behind. They all went upstairs to get ready for bed. "I guess we'll have to wait until another day to find our parents," Mary said.

Chapter Seventeen – The True Story

The following evening at dinner, Mary noticed the countess didn't come to eat. "Where's your mother?" she asked Katherine.

"I do not know. When father is away she often eats in her room."

"Do you think we could go visit her after we are done eating?" Mary asked.

"She would probably enjoy a visit from us. We should probably tell her you are back. I know she worried about you."

Mary enjoyed the meal, but tried to eat fast so that she would have time to visit with The Countess of Warwick. She whispered to John where she would be and then the two girls quickly slipped away. Katherine knocked at her mother's door and the girls waited for an answer. When they entered the room, the countess' seemed pleased to see them. "Did you have your dinner?" Katherine inquired.

"Yes I did. I am so glad to see that your friend has returned. How are my daughter and her dear friend this evening?"

Mary bowed to the lady. "You are looking well, Lady Beauchamp."

"Thank you, and thank you both for coming. I get lonely when I stay in my room, but sometimes when father is away it is too draining to get all dressed up for appearance sake."

"Do you want to go for a walk in the garden?" Katherine asked.

"No, I would rather stay here. It would be too big an effort to dress for a walk, although I am sure it is a lovely evening outside."

"How about a game of checkers?" Katherine asked.

"No, let us just sit and visit with one another. It is rare for me to spend time with you. I would also like to get to know your friend, Mary."

"Mary, can I tell my mother about what you told me yesterday?"

"Uh . . . I suppose that would be okay, if you don't think it will upset her too much."

"I doubt it will upset her, although I think she will have a hard time believing such an outlandish story as you have to tell."

Katherine started the story, and watched the countesses eyes grow large. "This is a strange story you are telling me," the countess said.

"I know it is, but I promise it's all true. We really do live in the future," Mary said. "I didn't tell Katherine this part, but you are my great-great-grandmother."

"Oh my goodness. Could that really be so?"

Mary shook her head. "Yes, I wouldn't pull your leg about something like that."

Katherine started to laugh. "You say the strangest things, Mary. I can hardly believe the things you say and I usually have no idea what they mean."

"I know," Mary said. "I'm always putting my foot in my mouth."

Katherine continued to laugh and soon her mother had joined her. "Are you laughing at me?" Mary asked.

"No, we are not. We are laughing at your strange words," Katherine said.

"Please continue with your story, Mary," the countess said.

Mary told her about the brooch her mother had shown her, and the story about how it had come into her possession. "So that is why you asked so many questions and wanted to see my beautiful pendant," The countess said.

"Yes, that is the reason," Mary said.

"Is this the only thing that your mother showed you?"

"Yes, that is as far as jewelry goes but we have the Beauchamp Coat of Arms hanging in our study."

"Is it the same one that we have hanging in our great hall?" Katherine asked.

"Yeah, it is, except the one you have is much larger."

Her great-great-grandmother seemed to be getting tired so Mary suggested that she and Katherine retire to their room. "We'll come and visit you again tomorrow," Mary said.

The countess nodded and told the girls to be careful and have a good night's rest and they left. "Do you think she believed me," Mary asked.

"Yes. I am sure she did," Katherine nodded. "I worry about what will happen to her if they do not release my father from prison soon."

"Do you think they are going to keep him?" Mary asked.

"I hope not, but treason is serious and I do not know how he is going to prove himself innocent. Everyone seems to believe the King."

Mary sat deep in thought and didn't say much the rest of the night. *I wonder if there is something that John or I could do to help him.*

Every night since she had returned from London Mary tossed and turned. Her dreams had been troubled with nightmares about her great-great-grandfather. She would just get to sleep and something would wake her up. She couldn't put her finger on what the problem could be. The next morning came much too early for Mary.

At breakfast, John asked Richard "Is there something we can do to help your father?"

Richard shook his head. "No there is not anything that anyone can do."

"We could break him out of prison," Mary said.

"No, do not even think such a thing," Richard said. "If they caught you they would probably behead you."

Mary grasped her throat. "They would do something like that to me?"

"Yes, they would. I have heard of them killing lots of children and women. They do not care if they think you did something wrong. They act and then ask questions."

"Oh, my," Mary said. "I guess we'll just have to hope that someone can prove him innocent soon."

"Mary, did you forget the story in the family book?" John asked.

"What story?" Mary asked.

"The one where we know that he is set free."

"You know that for sure?" Richard asked.

"Yes," John said. "Your father goes free."

"I wish I could see into the future," Richard said.

"Sometimes it does come in handy," John said.

"What are we going to do today?" Katherine asked.

"I thought that we would look for the secret passageway again," Mary said.

"Yes we will," Richard agreed.

"Maybe we should ask mother what she knows about hidden doors." Katherine suggested.

Richard agreed, "But we will have to wait for her to wake up. I would not want to disturb her too early."

"Let's go outside and see if we can come up with a place that looks similar to the one where they had the Ghost Alive Tour. Surely the castle hasn't changed that much in the last six hundred years," John said. "The next thing we were going to do after we finished the ghost tour was go watch a jousting match over on the island. I don't suppose there is any chance of us doing that today is there?"

"Actually, if you will put off looking for the secret door for a while we could go outside and watch the squires and knights practicing. They do that every day about this time," Richard said.

"Really?" John asked.

Richard nodded his head. "Yes they really practice every day. Father does not believe in letting them get rusty. Being prepared is important to him."

"Hurry up girls," John said.

"Oh, they can meet us there," Richard said looking at Katherine. "She knows the way. See you ladies after while."

With that the guys left the girls to finish their meal. "It really is quite fun to watch," Katherine said.

"I hate fighting."

"But this is not really fighting. They are only pretending to fight."

"Okay, I guess that will be okay. We don't have to stay a long time do we?"

"No. But it may be hard to get the men away from there once it starts," Katherine said.

"How long does it last?"

"Usually they only practice about an hour and I am sure they have already started, so we will not have to stay long."

"Okay, I'm ready," Mary said.

On the way Mary asked, "How does a man become a knight?"

"It is a long process and starts when a boy is only six or seven years old. They did not send Richard away because we already lived here at the castle. My father trained him. First he had to learn to dress my father and put on his armor. They played training games such as wrestling, piggy-back wrestling, and most days they practiced with blunt wooden swords and tiny round shields called bucklers. They also practiced with a lance on a rolling log pulled by two pages toward a target on one end of a swinging board. On the other end is a bag full of sand. When the lance hits the target the rider ducks or the huge bag will hit him on the back or head. Richard did not have to learn to read or write because he only had to learn knightly things."

"I had no idea that it involved so much work," Mary said.

"It does, Richard had to wait on my father and mother and he had to accompany them at all times. He learned how to hunt and hawk. When my father's armor got rusty, Richard rolled it in a barrel of sand until the rust disappeared. They taught him to be quick, graceful, and flexible. The chaplain gave him religious training, and sometimes he received training-in-arms from the squires."

"What is a squire?" Mary asked.

"When Richard turned fourteen, he became a squire. They appointed him to be a personal servant to one of the knights. In battle, he would bring his knight replacements of lances, swords, horses, or any other item that got lost or damaged in a battle. He had to become accustomed to heavy armor."

"Richard played games with real weapons against real knights. He learned to ride his war horse while keeping his weapon arm free. While a squire they allowed him to carry a sword and a shield, which showed what rank he had achieved. They taught him not to kill many knights. Most knights held other knights for ransom. Before he could become a knight he had to pray all night without sleeping or eating. When morning came he took a nice, warm bath. Then he put on a special padded vest and hood so that his armor did not hurt him. A page helped him put on chain mail armor. Then he had to put on a white tunic."

"Why did it have to white?" Mary asked.

"White is the color of peace, it also keeps the armor from rusting in the rain and sun. Next Richard knelt before my father, and father slapped him with the flat of the sword while he said,'I dub thee Sir Knight.' Then Richard received his sword, lance, and golden spurs."

"I had no idea that Richard was a knight," Mary said.

"Yes he is. My parents did not leave us girls out. While he trained, we girls all had to learn table manners, until we made no mistakes."

"You really do have good manners. Girls where I live do not have any idea the proper way to act at a dinner table."

The girls continued to talk as they walked to the island. They could see a large crowd of spectators watching as two men inside a ring went round and round waiting for the other one's move. Mary enjoyed watching because now she understood what each of these men did. She understood that they needed to practice in preparation of what lie ahead in their life.

After the practice the boys joined them and they walked across the bridge and back toward the castle.

"You didn't tell us that you are a knight," Mary said looking at Richard. "I guess that is why you rode in the front as we all went to London to see your father. I wondered why you wore that armor."

Richard looked at Katherine," Why did you have to tell her?"

"She had lots of questions, and I only wanted to tell her what I knew."

"Here we are friends, and you didn't even tell me," John said staring at Richard. "Why wouldn't you share that kind of information? That is really cool. You could show me lots of neat stuff."

"There you go again, talking about things I have no clue what they mean."

John laughed. "Sorry, our slang is so different than the language here. I just mean that it's really a good thing and there are things you could teach me. Can you teach me some of the things you had to learn?"

"You will be sorry. Some of the stuff is really hard and not much fun. I was probably luckier than most boys because my father taught me," Richard said.

"Or maybe unlucky because he taught you," Katherine said. "He was probably harder on you than someone else would have been."

"Maybe some of the time, but in the end I always knew that he loved me. So no matter how hard he made me work, I knew he cared."

"Make him learn that thing with the lance on a rolling log," Mary said.

Richard stopped and turned to Katherine. "You told her about that?"

"Yes, it is part of your training. I explained everything I could remember."

"I cannot believe you would do that," Richard said turning toward John. "It is fun and you will probably enjoy it as long as you make sure the sandbag does not hit you. After we search for the hidden door, we will go out to the practice area and I will show you a few things.

Chapter Eighteen – The Little Girl

By now they were back at the front of the castle. Mary and John stopped and searched the entire layout. "What do you think, Mary?" John said. "Where do you think we were when we climbed the hill for the ghost walk?"

Mary walked back and forth along the front of the castle. She stopped at several different spots and just shook her head. "Nothing seems quite right," she said.

John followed her and agreed. The two stopped and spoke with one another trying to decide on a spot that they both agreed could have been the path leading up to the tour. "Well, I know it had to be on the right side of the castle," Mary said.

"Yeah, you're right, but there isn't a hill there."

Richard walked over to the right side and pointed, "You mean up there?"

"Yeah," Mary said. "Nothing else stood on the right of me as we went up the hill."

"Maybe it is on the other side," Katherine suggested.

"I don't think so," John said. "The rest of the castle looks the same, but there isn't a hill or steps leading upward."

"What's up there?" Mary asked pointing to the top of the castle.

Katherine shook her head. "I have never been in that part of the castle, but we could probably go inside and go there. I love to explore new things."

"Yes. That is what we should do," Richard said.

The four went in the door nearest the great hall. They took the spiral staircase up to the highest level. The higher they climbed the tighter the circle became and the steps became narrower. Each step was barely wide enough for one foot. Next they made a right turn down the hall. When they came to a dead-end they went back to the adjoining hall and took it.

They had to make lots of detours because many of the hallways just stopped. Richard took them through many rooms that adjoined one another and they kept going the direction Mary had indicated. "This place needs a lot of work," Katherine said. "I wonder if mother and father know what bad shape it is in."

"I doubt it. They probably have not been up here in years. That is if they have ever been here," Richard said.

"If I had a place this big I would explore every nook and cranny," Mary said.

Richard laughed. "There you go again, speaking your own little language."

"Sorry," Mary said.

"It is okay," Richard said. "I actually enjoy listening to the way you talk. It makes me smile."

"Thanks," Mary said. "I love listening to you and Katherine. Your accent is the coolest."

Both Richard and Katherine laughed. "This has been the best time I have had for a long time," Katherine said. "With you here, Mother is not making me do all those dumb things I usually have to do every day. She lets me spend my time with you."

Finally, the four came to the end of the hall with no place else to go. Mary looked out the window. "I think we're at the end of the castle." This has to be where we were."

The group gathered around. "Maybe we didn't go this high up," John said.

"You might be right," Mary agreed, "But let's look around while we are here. Especially inspect the room right here."

Mary hurried inside the room and stepped to the wall and started tapping, looking for something unusual about it. She felt the entire wall and nothing seemed to change. The other three also inspected the entire wall. Nothing. Standing back she said, "Well, it can't be the wall where the window is or the one on that side because that's the outside. I guess it could be that other one where the door is that we came in through, but I don't think this is the right place.

John looked at his watch, "I don't think so either and it's past time for the mid-day meal so I think we should call it a day. I need some food and then Richard has to teach me something."

Discouraged they found their way back downstairs. "We're never going to find Mom and Dad again," Mary said.

"Yes, you will," Richard said. "We will not stop until we do. What are you and Katherine going to do for the rest of the day?"

Mary shrugged. "I don't know. Maybe I'll have her teach me some of that fancy needlework stuff. My mom would really be impressed if I learned to do something like that. She's tried to teach me several times, but it doesn't hold my interest for long."

Richard chuckled. "Katherine seems to enjoy it, but maybe that is because she had to learn to do it at an early age. While I learned to be a knight she had to learn needlework, gardening, and lots of ridiculous things."

"They were not ridiculous. Mother told me that every lady has to know how to run a castle like this. It is not an easy task, and takes lots of skills that even you do not have," Katherine said sticking her tongue out at her brother.

This surprised Mary. She had honestly thought that it was only her and John that did dumb things like that. She couldn't contain herself she did a victory dance right there in front of everyone. "I can't believe that brothers and sisters living in the fourteenth century don't get along. I can hardly wait to tell mom. It isn't just John and I that don't get along."

* * *

After the meal, the boys left in a hurry. John could hardly wait to learn some of the skills the knights had to learn. Katherine and Mary talked the countess into working with them on some sewing items. Katherine excused herself to retrieve the items they would need and Mary walked with her great-grandma to a comfortable bench in the garden.

When Katherine returned with her two younger sisters, Margaret and Elizabeth they also brought their sewing items along so their mother could help them. Katherine showed Mary an attractive drawstring pouch that held a thimble, a wooden needle case with some white cow bone needles about two inches long, as well as something Katherine called a snip. Mary knew they used it in the same way she used a pair of scissors. As Katherine pulled out her handiwork, Mary gasped. "I had no idea that you knew how to do embroidery."

The countess nodded her head. "We have been doing this in my family for years. I understand that all the women of nobility learn this exquisite art. I have often wondered if the reason was to keep us busy since we live in a castle isolated from people. It certainly helps me to relax and sitting here in this beautiful garden is the best medicine for an old lady."

"I never thought of you as being an old lady," Mary said. "You are charming and still have many years ahead of you."

"Thank you, my dear, Mary. That is kind of you," the countess said.

"So, Mary do you know how to embroider?" Katherine asked.

"Yeah, I thought all girls learned how to do this," Mary answered.

"I think it is only the wealthy or those from nobility that master it. The others are probably too busy working in the fields, gardens, or kitchens. I brought a piece of fabric for you to work on," Katherine said handing it to Mary.

"My mom will certainly be surprised if I actually sit still long enough to learn to do anything. I love creating something attractive, but I lack the patience to ever finish it. After it is done the beautiful raised designs with threads are something to admire. My mother is really great at this, but I sure haven't developed that talent yet."

As all the girls and the countess sat in the garden they enjoyed the sunshine and the comfortable talk. The sisters and their mother often laughed at the ideas that came out of Mary's mouth. "I heard they did embroidery even before painting. Probably some cave wife discovered she could lace hides together with strips of leather in a different pattern and make it look different and probably quite lovely. When she did this her husband could pick out his own hide from all the others."

Katherine laughed, "You are such a dreamer."

"This isn't the first time I've been accused of that," Mary said.

Looking up from her masterpiece, Mary noticed the boys headed their way. John limped and didn't move very fast. Mary set her sewing aside and rushed to his side. "What happened?"

"Nothing, I'm fine," John said.

"No you aren't. I can see you have been hurt. Come and sit down."

Richard helped John to the bench and then turned to explain to his mother what had happened. "He did real well on the log the first few times, but then he slipped and the bag of sand slammed into him real hard."

"Is that how he scraped his face?" the countess asked. "Katherine, run to the kitchen for help. Bring some water and a rag to clean the wound, and bring someone with you that will know how to nurse John properly."

Mary sat next to John and put her arm around her brother, trying to comfort him, but he kept pushing her arm away. "Just leave me alone. I will be fine."

Mary took her arm away, but stayed nearby. She felt relief when she saw Katherine coming with a couple of women following close behind. John hated the fuss they made over him, but because they were strangers, he kept his mouth shut. Mary could tell he hurt because as they cleaned his face he flinched several times. She really wanted to laugh at him because of his clumsiness, but knew she shouldn't.

As soon as the countess knew that John had been taken care of she reminded everyone that they needed to prepare for the evening meal. She then left to go to her room. "Did you have fun?" Mary asked John.

"Yeah, I really did. Richard showed me lots of cool tricks and until I slipped I loved it."

Mary nodded. "I'm glad you had a great time. Do you think you'll ever be good enough to be a Knight?"

Richard laughed. "It will take a lot longer than one day to learn all the things he needs to know, but he did quite well for only a few hours of instructions."

They all knew they didn't want to be late for dinner so they went to their rooms to change. Mary noticed that John still limped, and wondered what else he had done to hurt himself, but she thought it best to not ask any more questions about his injury. In fact, she thought it best if she left the entire accident alone.

* * *

Mary felt extremely tired, and as soon as dinner was finished she went to the bedroom. Shortly after nodding off to sleep, she heard a little girl crying. She quickly sat up and looked around but after not noticing anything in the dark she laid back down as she reached for her flashlight. Even though she was exhausted, she still had trouble going back to sleep. She lay awake waiting for the girl to start crying again. Finally, she could hold her eyes open no longer, and fell asleep.

About midnight the crying started again. Mary sat up, and wiped the sleep from her eyes. She listened closely and could hear the crying come down the spiral staircase toward her bedroom. Then she carefully rolled from her bed and grabbing her flashlight, she left the room and followed the sound. When she could hear the girl better, she carefully pointed the flashlight toward the floor and flipped it on. It gave enough light that she could watch where to go. *I wonder if I should talk to her,* Mary thought.

She followed the crying. *Where is she taking me?* Mary wondered.

Finally, Mary could stand it no longer, "What is the matter?" she whispered. "What can I do to help?"

The crying slowed, but Mary could still hear weeping although it had grown quieter. Mary continued to follow as they went down some more stairs. *I sure hope we aren't going to the dungeon.*

After they reached the lower floor where the servants worked and slept, the sound moved toward the kitchen. Just as Mary reached to open the door, she heard another door in another part of the house slam. Immediately, she knew the young girl had disappeared. Mary thought she had heard someone else wandering around the castle. She turned off her flashlight and waited. After a long time she decided she must have been hearing things because she never saw anyone or heard another noise again. Mary headed back toward the bedroom, and back to bed. Exhausted she soon fell asleep.

The next morning the girls met the boys outside their bedroom door. John looked at Mary and asked, "What's wrong with you? You look like a train ran over you."

"I didn't sleep very well. All night long, I could hear a little girl crying. Did you hear anything?"

"Nope."

"What about you Katherine, did you hear that little girl that cried almost all night long?" Mary asked.

Katherine shook her head. "Sorry, I did not hear a thing. I must have been too tired."

Mary looked at Richard. "Once I am asleep I do not hear anything," he said.

Finally, Mary really looked at John and she could tell he hadn't slept well. "Are you okay?" she asked.

John nodded his head. "Yeah, just a little stiff."

"And sore," Mary added.

"How can you tell?"

"That's easy, you can hardly move."

Mary followed John down the stairs. "I bet this is one time you wish they had elevators."

"Please don't make me laugh, Mary. That really hurts the ribs."

"Do you think you broke them?" Mary asked.

"I don't know, but Richard helped me bind them last night before we went to bed."

"That's good. Are you going to feel like exploring today?"

"Nothing would stop me from that. The sooner we get home, the happier I'm going to be," John declared.

Mary laughed. "You mean you don't want to be a Knight?"

"I doubt I could get through the training."

Mary almost skipped to breakfast. She could feel her stomach growling and knew soon others would hear the loud rumble. After eating Katherine asked, "Are we still going to go looking for the secret door?"

"I am," Mary said.

John nodded, "I'm ready any time you are."

Chapter Nineteen – Another Meeting

This time Katherine and Mary took the lead and the guys followed close behind. They planned to go to third floor and proceed to the far end below where they had finished the day before. There had to be miles and miles of hallways and a mass of corridors that led from one area to the next. Would their search ever be over?

Next they would check everything along the front end of the castle. "Wow, it doesn't look like anyone has been up here for a long time," Mary said.

"I doubt that anyone ever comes up here. We only use rooms on the second floor and then the main one. The servants are usually only in the lower level."

Mary ran her fingers along the wall, and came away with lots of dust. "What used to be up here?"

Katherine shrugged her shoulders and turned toward the guys who trailed a long ways. As they approached she asked, "Richard, what used to be up here?"

"I have never been here. Usually if we went exploring we went outside to one of the towers. I thought you girls would have been up here."

"Not me," Katherine said. "I just liked to explore all the rooms near my bedroom. I did not need to come up here for adventure."

"Did you notice that the rooms on this floor all have heavy wooden doors with massive locks?" John asked.

"This one's not locked," Mary said as she pushed open a door and stepped inside. A wooden rocking horse with faded paint stood in one corner. At the other end of the room sat some building blocks. Story books were scattered along the floor in front of a small shelf. A twin bed covered with a handmade quilt sat in the far corner.

"Was this your nursery?" Mary asked.

"I do not remember ever being here," Katherine answered.

After looking around the room and pounding on the walls the two girls closed the door and continued on down the hall. At last the girls came to a dead end. "Well, this is as far as we can go," Mary said. "Now we can start checking out all the inside walls from here back to the staircase."

No one really talked, they kept busy knocking on walls and searching for indentations that would mean they had found a hidden doorway. Disappointed, the four met at the top of the stairs. "Wow we wasted a lot of time," John said.

"Well, we can go back and check the rear side or we can go down and check the floor our bedrooms are on." Richard said.

"I am sick of all the dust," Katherine said.

"Let's go down and see what we can see below," John suggested.

"That will not do us any good because my sisters and I use to play there all the time," Katherine said.

"Yeah, but you didn't look for anything special," Mary said.

"You are right, we only played."

Mary wanted to slide down the banister, but after watching John she decided against it. He still had a hard time even walking, and she shouldn't remind him of how bad he really felt. The group of four walked past the bedrooms and continued to the end of the hall. This time it didn't have an abrupt end, it circled around and then the hall continued back the way they had come except on the back side of the castle. Each side of the hall had rooms with their own separate doors. "This is nice," Mary said. "Maybe we should start from here and work our way back to the bedrooms, and then do the other side of the castle later."

They all agreed on the plan and the boys took one side of the hallway while the girls took the front side. The girls finished first and didn't find anything along the way. However, when almost finished they heard the boys calling, "Hey, you two. Come see what we found."

The two girls ran as quickly as they could to the room where the boys were. "It is another hidden door," Richard said. "It goes from this room into the next one. I wish I had this bedroom."

"You mean it doesn't go into the dark tunnel?" Mary asked.

"Nope, but at least we know there are other doors leading from one room to another," Richard said.

Katherine stopped and looked at the doorway from both the rooms, and then she went into the hall. This is exactly the same distance from father's room as the door in the library and music room are from his door, but this one is going this way and the other one is headed the other direction. Do you think that has any significance?"

"Are you sure there isn't another door on the inside wall?" Mary asked.

The four of them checked every inch of the inside wall, but found nothing there. "I think we missed lunch," John said.

"What?" Richard asked.

"Oh, I mean the mid-day meal," John said.

"What time does your watch say?" Mary asked.

"It's almost two o'clock."

"Will they still let us eat?" Mary asked.

Katherine laughed. "Of course, all we have to do is tell one of the servants that we are hungry. Come on, let us go downstairs."

Once they sat at a table, it didn't take Katherine long to find a servant to bring them some food. The four of them talked about the trip to London and the way Mary had fooled everyone. They were all sad because no word had come about the Earl. When they had finished, Mary turned toward Richard, "What are you going to do this afternoon?"

"Since it appears that John is hurting too much for any training, I thought I would take him over to watch some of the others while they are being instructed. It is something I think he would enjoy."

"Yeah, Richard, that sounds fun as long as I'm not the one in the way of those heavy bags."

With that, both boys laughed as they bid the girls goodbye. "Have a fun day," John called.

"What do you want to do today," Katherine asked.

"Let's not sew. I had enough of that yesterday," Mary said watching Katherine's face. "Not that I didn't have fun, because I did, but I'm used to being busier than that."

"What would you do if you were home?"

"I'd probably be on the computer, or out riding my horse."

"What is a computer?"

"Oh, there I go again. It's very complicated. I usually play games on it, or talk to friends on Facebook or Twitter, or sometimes I do homework on it.

"It must be one of those contraptions that you cannot use here. Sounds complicated to me. Let us go riding," Katherine said. "I am sure there are extra horses around that no one is using today. I will check with the stable hand and see what he says."

"Okay. That would be fun," Mary said.

"I thought after your trip to London you would be tired of riding horses."

"No, I could ride every day. My dad says that he thinks I was born on a horse."

"My brothers are the ones who usually got to go riding. My mother expected us girls to learn sewing and cooking skills. I never understood why because we have plenty of servants to do those things."

"Maybe it's just so you will learn how to sew and cook. That's what my mom usually tells me when I grumble about learning something new. She says, 'You'll never know when it will come in handy so you need to learn how to do it'," Mary said.

"I have never thought of it that way," Katherine said.

"My mom tells us all the time about things she had to do when her and my dad first got married. It must have been hard because she had always helped with things in the house and she had no idea how to weed a garden or what to do with the animals. The stories about her learning to
gather the eggs are choice."

"I doubt I will ever have to cook anything, but I guess it is good I know how," Katherine said. "I do not think my father would ever let me marry below my station in life. I will probably always have servants."

"What does it mean to marry below your station?"

"My father would never allow me to get married unless the one I marry is of nobility. He would have to be heir to a fortune and I will always live in a castle such as this."

"Wow," Mary said. "Things don't work that way back in the United States. There are no castles, and I guess there are some wealthy people, I just don't know any of them. I will marry anyone I choose."

"You get to choose the one you want to marry?" Katherine asked.

"Yeah, that is if I ever meet someone I like, if he asks me to marry him I can. Of course, I would hope my parents at least like him."

"My parents will pick for me. I probably will not even know the man I marry until after I am married."

"That would be awful," Mary said.

"My mother did not know my father until after the wedding. I think she may have seen him at a distance while at a ball one night, but she never met him officially. It worked out for them, and I think it will be good for me."

"You mean that your mother married someone she didn't even know?"

"Yes, she did."

"You don't get to go on dates?" Mary asked.

"I do not know what that means."

"Where I come from when you turn sixteen a boy can ask a girl on a date," Mary explained. "They either go to the movies, or a dance, or maybe just to get some ice cream."

"That all sounds strange to me," Katherine said. "I do not know what I would do if I had to go somewhere with a boy other than my own brother. What is a movie?"

Mary laughed. "There I go again talking about things that you have no idea about and things that I don't know how to explain."

The two girls arrived at the barn and asked about borrowing some horses so they could go for a ride. The man in the stable seemed a little bit reluctant because never had Katherine requested such a thing. "You better be careful," he told her.

"We will," Katherine assured him.

"Your father would probably not want you to go far," he said. "Maybe you should stay on the castle grounds. I would not want anything to happen to you, Miss."

"I could help you," Mary said.

"No, ma'am. This is my job, and I will do it."

Mary stood back and watched him put the side saddle on Katherine's horse. She knew she could probably do it in half the time it took him. Not wanting to ride that way she quickly mounted her horse before he could saddle it. Katherine sat as a lady should and Mary sat on the horse the way that men do. Katherine raised her eyebrows when she saw Mary, but she didn't say anything. Mary noticed the stableman also looked at her strangely, but he also didn't speak. Mary followed Katherine, not sure which direction to go. After they had left the castle behind, she pulled aside Katherine hoping that they could at least talk while they rode.

"Is it okay that I ride like this," Mary asked.

"Of course, why would it not be?" Katherine asked.

"The way that man looked at me I thought that maybe I should sit like you. Is it not proper for me to ride this way?"

"He just does not know you, but I have come to realize that your ways are much different than mine. Most everything you do any more does not surprise me."

"I don't mean to offend or hurt anyone," Mary said, "but this is the way I usually ride at home."

"You must know that you do not offend me. I quite like the things you do. It shows me that you are independent. I do not know if I will ever be like you, but I do admire you and your ways," Katherine said.

"Let's go to the end of the castle property this way and then you can show me how far it goes that direction," Mary pointed.

"Instead, I will race you to the river," Katherine said as she dug her heels in before Mary could respond.

"Hey, that's cheating. Wait for me," Mary yelled as she nudged her horse to follow.

The horse's gait was smooth and Mary felt as though she flew through the air. She followed close behind Katherine over the hills and through the forests until at last Mary could see the river.

"What was that?" Mary asked when something whizzed by her head. She ducked her head and pulled her horse to a stop.

"Oh, that is nothing to worry about; probably Marvin is out training the birds again."

"What kind of birds?"

"Falcons," Katherine answered. "We can continue on because I do not think it will hurt you."

"But can't we watch?" Mary asked.

"Yes, if you want to."

"I do, the only time I've ever seen a bird like this was in a zoo. Whoops, I'm sorry I'm sure you have no idea what a zoo is."

Katherine laughed.

Mary turned the horse toward the area where a man held his gloved hand up for a bird to land. She had never seen anyone try this before. The wings on the bird were long and thin and tapered into a point. It had dark blue-gray wings and a black back with a light underside. She could hardly make out its white face but could tell it had a black stripe on its cheek. As the man turned toward the girls he waved, and held the bird up. Its large dark eyes looked right at Mary, making her shiver. The falcon made a kek-kek-keh noise and lifted into the air. As the girls watched, it increased its speed and then quickly changed direction. They watched as its half-closed foot grabbed a small bird in mid-air, and soon it flew back to the man. Mary had never seen a bird fly so fast.

"Come with me, and I will introduce you to Marvin," Katherine said.

The trainer nodded to the two girls as the rode their horses close to him. "Good day, Lady Katherine," he said turning toward Katherine. "What are you doing way out here?"

"My friend Mary and I wanted to take a ride. This is the first time that she has seen a bird such as this up close."

"Climb off from the horse, and I will let you hold it," Marvin said.

Mary watched Katherine and sat very still, not sure if she wanted to get off from the safety of the horse. When she didn't move Katherine asked, "Are you going to come and see the bird?"

She shook her head and sat quietly and watched. "I'm not sure. You hold it first and I'll see. Maybe in a minute I will."

The bird didn't stay on Katherine's hand for long. It soon soared through the air again. "Are these the only birds you train?" Mary asked.

"No. We keep other birds here. There is a magnificent eagle, a few vultures, hawks, and an owl that I think you would like."

Mary watched the outstanding show the bird put on as it glided around the sky above. "I don't think I want to hold the bird today, but can we come again? I would love to meet the owl. It is probably not as intimidating as that falcon is."

Marvin laughed. "It does take some getting used to. Katherine has been here before and is acquainted with the birds."

Katherine climbed back onto her horse and the two galloped away with Mary still watching the bird above. "That is a nice man, but I don't envy his job," Mary said. "I bet those birds have hurt him a few times."

"Maybe, but I think they are pretty tame now."

"That could be, but I'm not sure I would trust that bird. Did you see the way he wrapped those claws around that poor little bird?"

"You are probably right, but they have never hurt me. I do not think Marvin would let me hold it if he thought the bird is dangerous," Katherine said.

"Yeah, you are right. Your parents would be furious with him if any harm came to you," Mary agreed. "How much further to the end of the property?"

"I think it is just over that hill."

The two rode in comfortable silence each deep in their own thoughts. Mary longed to be home, yet she loved the peace she found here at this ancient castle. It had been a long time since she had felt this way. In her world there was always so many places to go and way too much to do. Here these people took the time to communicate. Besides visiting with one another, Richard and Katherine always seemed to have leisure time, something that her life lacked.

Mary tried to map out in her mind the sort of changes she needed to make so that her life could be calmer. Maybe she could stop some of her after school activities this coming school year. She didn't have to belong to all those clubs. Mary didn't have to keep up with the Jones' or in her case, all the other girls. She needed to only do those things that would bring her real pleasure.

When had her world gotten so complicated? Her mother had discouraged her from doing so much, but she never stopped her from doing the things that she wanted to. Her mother's policy seemed right. She believed that she should let her children do their own thing and she shouldn't force her wants upon her children. *I bet she gets tired of driving me all over the place,* Mary thought as she resolved to change things when she got back home. That is, if she ever got back to her old life.

As they neared the top of the hill, Mary anxiously wanted to see what was on the other side and spurred her horse forward at a faster pace. "There's the wall," she called to Katherine. "I can see the end of the property."

Katherine caught up to Mary and the two reined in their horses and stared ahead. "This is magnificent," Mary said. "Things in Utah are never this green."

"Maybe it does not rain as much there as it does here."

"You are right. It does rain a lot in England."

"Now are you ready to go that direction?" Katherine asked pointing to her left. "We don't have to go the other way because you can see from here how far it is."

"Can't we stop and rest for a few minutes? I need to stretch my legs," Mary said.

The two dismounted and took their horses reins and started walking. "This is a beautiful day," Katherine said. "I will sure miss you when you leave."

"Yup. It is a gorgeous day. Maybe you can go back home with me," Mary suggested.

"That sounds like a fun adventure, but I do not think it would be possible."

"But what if it was?" Mary asked.

"I think I would be afraid that if I went I might not be able to return again. I also think that I would not fit into your world."

"I would teach you everything you need to know."

Katherine shook her head. "It would be too overwhelming to me. I like my life here, and I love my parents and would miss them if I left," Katherine said.

Mary didn't know what to say. She knew that Katherine was right. Her world would be too complicated for Katherine. She really would be better off here in her own castle. Besides why would anyone want to give up living in a castle to live in a busy city where she had to go to school every day and do chores. Katherine had it made, she had servants to wait on her, and she could almost have anything she wanted. Yeah, she didn't have any of the modern day conveniences, but she had a better world with knights in shining armor. Katherine really did have a Cinderella life.

Finally, Mary nodded. "You're right Katherine, your life here would be much better for you. I am just being selfish and wanted to take you home so that I'd have a really great friend. None of my friends are anything like you."

"Thanks Mary, I think you are a great friend too, but you are so much smarter than me. I would never fit in your world."

"I understand that now, but it's not because I'm any smarter than you are, it is just things are way different in Utah than they are here."

The two girls climbed back on the horses and rode them until they were almost all the way around, then Mary said, "I bet it's almost dinner time. My stomach is rumbling again."

"You are probably right. I think you have seen almost everything so we better head back to the stable. I doubt they will want to wait dinner for us."

It didn't take long for the girls to arrive and less time to unsaddle Katherine's horse. Of course, they didn't get to finish the job because the stableman hurried to their sides before they could finish. The girls quickly went inside and up the stairs to their room. After changing they dashed downstairs. They couldn't find the boys so they found a place where they could watch for their arrival. Mary anxiously waited for them. She wanted to eat and had lots of questions about their afternoon.

After they arrived, they insisted on going to their room and changing for dinner. John said he wouldn't answer any questions until he had something to eat. Once the four had their meal in front of them Mary almost didn't give them time to answer one question before asking another one. Finally, John had enough and told her, "Stop monopolizing the entire conversation."

"I'm sorry," Mary said and ducked her head. "I just wanted to know what you two had been doing all afternoon."

She didn't talk for awhile and listened as Richard started asking John about where he lived. "So, tell me again where you are from," Richard said.

"I'm from America, or some people call it the United States of America."

"I've never heard of the United States of America."

"No, you wouldn't have," John said. "It didn't exist for at least another hundred years. If I remember correctly, Christopher Columbus discovered the Americas in 1492. He sailed on a ship called the Santa Maria, and proved the world is round. Every year in October we celebrate his discovery."

"So you believe the world is round and that is when your country was founded?" Richard asked.

"Yes, the world is round, and no, the founding of our country didn't happen until after the Pilgrims came."

"What are the Pilgrims?"

Mary butted in, "They sailed from England in 1620 seeking religious freedom."

"Besides Columbus discovered America in the south and the pilgrims landed in the north," John said.

"The history of your country is sure complicated," Richard said.

"To us it isn't, but we've grown up hearing the stories all of our lives," Mary said. "The saddest story I know is when we fought the British for Independence."

"You mean our country and your country fought against one another?" Katherine asked.

Both John and Mary nodded. "That doesn't make us enemies though," Mary said. "Our countries are friends with one another now."

"I am sure glad of that," Katherine said.

"Well, I'm tired," Mary said. "We had a long ride today and if I want to get up and continue our search tomorrow I better get to bed."

The other three agreed and they all climbed the stairs to their rooms. Mary really hoped that tomorrow would be a successful day. She felt they were running out of time and she wanted to go home. Most of all she wanted to see her parents again.

Chapter Twenty – Punishment

The next morning came a little too early for Mary, and as she attempted to get out of bed every muscle in her body ached. *It must be from all the tossing and turning to get the little girl's cries out of my head.*

"Come on, you need to get up," Katherine urged. "My mother always tells me that once I am up and moving around I will feel better."

"Yeah, I know. That's what my mom also says, but I don't want too," Mary moaned. "I think I rode too long yesterday."

"I thought you were used to riding a horse."

"I am, but when I'm in school I don't have much time to ride because I have so many other things going on in my life. I'm lucky if I even have time on Saturday. I think poor Prince feels neglected. As soon as school was out we left on this vacation."

"I am so sorry you are so sore, but I know that once you are up and moving around you will feel better."

"Yeah, I know."

With that, Mary rolled over and pushed herself into a sitting position. "I just know that today is the day we are going to be lucky."

"I think you are right. There really cannot be any other place to look. This has to be the day," Katherine agreed.

They continued chatting as they dressed for the day. Mary took extra care in making sure that she looked just right. Then she dumped out her backpack and checked to make sure she had everything. She had her clothes, and jacket. Also her flashlight, but she quickly took it out and handed it to Katherine. "We are going to need this today."

Of course, she had her phone because she hadn't had any reason to use it. She used the brush on her hair and then placed it back into her bag. After putting on some lip gloss she also put that inside the backpack. Mary also put her fingernail clippers, emery board, and lotion in their proper place. She grabbed the lotion and applied a large amount. Then she reached for Katherine's hands and rubbed some onto them. "What is this?" Katherine asked.

"It's some lotion to help keep your hands soft."

"It feels wonderful, and the smell is delicious."

After the girls had rubbed on a sufficient amount of lotion Mary placed it back into the bag. She then counted her books and made sure she had all her scriptures, paper and pens. "I think I have everything, but maybe I better look around the room to make sure I didn't leave anything."

"You act like you are not going to be coming back here," Katherine said.

Mary stopped her search and looked toward Katherine. "Well, if we find the secret passageway, I won't be staying here any longer, I'll be going home."

Katherine didn't say anything she just sat on the bed. Mary moved things around in her bag trying to make the weight even on each side so that it would be easier to carry. Finally, realizing that Katherine hadn't said anything for a while she turned around. She couldn't believe her eyes. Katherine had tears sliding down her face. "Oh, Katherine, I'm sorry," Mary said running to her side. "Don't cry."

"But I will miss you so much."

"I will miss you too, but I have to go home or my parents will be really upset."

Katherine nodded her head. "I know."

"Then don't cry any more, or I'll feel bad," Mary said. "My bag is packed so we better go eat breakfast. I'm starved."

Once again the boys had beat them there, but it didn't take the girls long to catch up. "Are you ready?" John asked Mary.

She nodded as she stood up ready to leave. "Today has to be our lucky day."

John stood up and the two high-fived high in the air. Katherine and Richard looked on, bewildered by the actions of their friends.

Embarrassed, Mary said, "Sorry."

They all hurried to the spiral stairs and climbed them quickly. This time they knew exactly where they wanted to go. It didn't take long for them to start banging on the walls. The secret door had to be here. They had to find it. The morning dragged on, and still no luck. Mary slid to the floor. "It has to be here," she said.

John agreed. "We will find it, but there has to be something we aren't looking for. Maybe it isn't hollow, like the other ones. What if it has something in the floor triggering it?"

Mary and John started crawling along the floor. Mary felt determined that she would find a way home. Every day she missed her parents a little more than the day before. She really liked Katherine, Richard, and their mom, but no one could replace her own mom and dad.

Richard kept close to the two friends but he inspected the walls. This time he didn't knock on them, he just felt up and down all the seams and tried to see if he could find anything different. Katherine followed the group, not sure what to do. "Are you sure about the location?" she asked.

Mary turned to look at her. "I think so, but I could be wrong."

Katherine left the little group and wandered around. Mary kept watching her, wondering what she thought about. John continued to crawl along the floor, but Mary stopped and sat very still, thinking. In her mind she went over the entire scene with her tripping and pulling John with her through the wall. She knew something was missing, but she couldn't put her finger on it. What else had happened? Then she did something that she hadn't done for awhile. She left the others and walked to a quiet corner and knelt to pray.

Mary finally joined the group again. "I just thought of something," she said.

After they gathered around she told them, "When I tripped and fell, I pulled John with me. We didn't end up immediately in the tunnel, we landed in something like a small closet, or a room as small as one."

They all slid to the floor. Mary deep in thought looked all around the room they were in. "None of the rooms have closets."

"What exactly are closets?" Richard asked.

"Oh, I forgot you don't have them here in the castle," Mary said. "At home each of our bedrooms has a small spot with a door on. Inside is a rod where we hang our clothes. On the floor I can put my shoes, and my backpack. In my closet, I also have shelves where I can store other stuff. We also have a closet downstairs where we hang our coats. Here you don't have any such enclosures except the one below the stairs by the servant's quarters, but we weren't by any stairs, and there wasn't much room for my head."

John shook his head. "I haven't seen any rooms that small."

"I know," Mary said. "But there has to be something that size."

Richard snapped his finger. "Maybe behind the fireplace or under some furniture there is a small hole where you can go from one floor to the other."

Slowly Mary nodded her head. "That does make sense. Maybe years ago they had to have a way they could slip out of their room and hide or escape so they wouldn't be caught."

"I know just the place to look," Richard said. "If we had a war going on, the first place the enemy would go is to the master's bedroom. They would be trying to slay the Earl of the castle. Once they captured or killed him, they could take possession of the entire place."

"But we looked in there," Katherine said.

"Not good enough. We didn't move any of the furniture or look behind father's fireplace. We only inspected the walls."

"Yeah, Richard, I think you're on to something," John said.

"Do you have any idea where mother is?" Katherine asked. "She will be really upset if we disturb any of father's things, so we will have to be real quiet."

"Why don't you and I go find your mother?" Mary said. "Maybe we can distract her somehow while the boys look over the room."

"Yes, we could make sure she is not in her room. As long as she is not close enough to hear us, we should be able to do anything we want," Katherine agreed.

"We'll come and get you as soon as the coast is clear," Mary told the boys.

They both nodded, and the girls ran down the hall wanting to make sure the countess didn't come anywhere close by. They found her as she neared the staircase. "I wondered where you ladies were," she said.

"I have just been showing Mary some more of the castle."

"That is nice. I hope you are not getting into any trouble. What are your plans for the rest of the day?"

"I thought Mary and I would see the rest of the rooms upstairs. She has never seen a castle before. Yesterday we went riding, but I think we are both a little stiff to do that again. Mary did not really like the sewing."

"Where are the boys?" Katherine's mother asked.

"I think they are doing some exploring also."

The countess nodded, and said, "I am going to sit in the garden for a while before time to eat. See you then."

Katherine and Mary waited for her mother to go outside before running up the stairs. They found the boys still sitting where they had left them and told them they could now go into the Earl's bedchambers. Once inside the boys first moved Richard's father's writing table. There was nothing there. Then they moved the chest where he kept his clothing. Still nothing. They both moved toward the fireplace. "If someone tried to escape through here in the winter time, I think they'd get a little hot," John said.

They still carefully inspected any possibility, but zilch, they found nothing. Then John crawled under the bed, but found nothing there. Richard asked John to help him move the head of the bed away from the wall. Both boys just stood still. They couldn't believe their eyes. Richard and Mary were right. They found a small partition in the wall. They hardly noticed the panel. To Mary it almost looked like a sliding door. They had finally found the secret compartment. It took the four of them many minutes to figure out the combination and get the door open.

With only enough room for a couple of them to get inside, they agreed to take turns inspecting the hideaway. Richard had to examine every little corner and Mary thought she would never get a turn. Then John studied every detail of the small enclosure. Next Katherine got to check it out. At long last Mary had a turn. "I think this is lots smaller than the one we were in," Mary said stepping inside.

"Are you sure?" Richard asked.

She had to look over everything once and then again. Mary nodded her head. "Yup, I've never been here before."

When she moved out of the small closet Richard asked, "We still have to check it out. Where do you think this will lead us?"

"I hope we don't end up in the tunnel," she said.

"Maybe it does not go anywhere," Katherine said.

"It has to go somewhere, or why would they have built it?" John asked.

"John is right. They would not build this compartment if it did not go somewhere," Richard said.

"Who is going to try to figure out how to get out of here?" Mary asked.

"I want to try it first," Richard said stepping back inside.

He ran his fingers all around the walls. "Come in here, John. What did you do to make the wall move?"

"I just pushed on it."

The two pushed on all three sides of the wall, but nothing budged. "I told you so," Mary said.

Then John stooped down to look at the floor and Richard reached high above his head to feel the ceiling. "Boost me up a little ways," he called to John.

Soon the entire ceiling moved and Richard pulled himself up. "Send up the girls first, they are shorter than you," Richard called.

After the four pulled themselves up, Richard told them to move over to the side so he could replace the board before anyone fell through the hole. They were all smashed into a larger closet. "This is it, John. This is where we were," Mary explained.

"Yup, this is it. That wall right there took us to the tunnel, so we don't want to push on it," John said.

Without much room the two girls stood out of the way and let the guys search for a way out of the room. John shook his head. "It doesn't make sense. Where is the door that will let us out of here?"

"What if it's only on the other side of the wall?" Mary asked.

"That should not be so hard," Richard said. "All we would have to do is go to the room above where father's bedchamber is and search it."

"So how do we get there?" Katherine asked.

"That's simple," John said. "We go back the way we came."

After they had climbed back down, they decided they better make an appearance at the mid-day meal or the countesses' feathers would be ruffled.

"This all makes sense to me," Richard said during the meal. "If my father ever gets in trouble, and he has any warning, he can escape from the King's men by going through that hole in his bedroom. He can easily escape through the tunnel."

"Maybe he does not know about the secret passageway," Katherine said.

"Yeah, if he doesn't know about it, he can't use it," Mary agreed.

"But he also couldn't use it if he didn't have time to get away," John said.

"Now, all I have to do is remember to tell him about it when he returns so he will always be safe," Richard said.

Mary kept busy throwing all her ideas around and she didn't even pay attention to what she ate. She didn't even notice that the countess watched all of them. Before they could leave, the countess stood over her children with her hands on her hips. "What are the two of you up to?"

Mary and John both ducked their heads. "Nothing Mother," Richard said.

"Do not tell me that. You are looking guilty and I want to know what you are going to do the rest of the day. Maybe you should spend some time with me in the garden weeding this afternoon."

A lump formed in Mary's throat. *Oh no, what are we going to do?* she wondered.

"But Mother, I have guests to entertain."

"They are big enough to look out for themselves or maybe the four of you should all join me. After all, if what Mary says is true they are relatives. We should not let those weeds get out of control. I have been far too lenient with you while Mary and John have been here. Every morning and afternoon you disappear, and leave me here alone. It is lonely without your father by my side."

"But Mother, Mary and I sewed with you a few days ago," Katherine said.

"Yes, you did. That helped pass the day faster, but yesterday you were gone all day. Now, there will be no argument from any of you," she said before turning and walking away.

The four looked at one another, and no one spoke for a long time. Finally John said, "I think we better hurry to your father's room and get that bed pushed back where it belongs before anyone discovers it."

"I'll cover for you two for a few minutes, but you better not be long," Mary said.

The girls strolled to the garden as slow as they could. Mary didn't know what kind of excuse she could come up with, but she knew it needed to be a good one. As soon as the countess saw them in the garden she immediately asked where the boys where. "Oh, they weren't finished with their meal yet, but they promised to hurry and they'll be here soon," Mary said looking around. "Where is the hoe and gardening gloves?"

Katherine looked at her as though she had grown horns, but it was too late to take back the words. The countess rose her eyebrows in question, "What did you ask me, dear?"

"Oh, nothing. Where do you want me to start pulling the weeds?"

"I think I am going to separate each of you so that you do not spend the entire afternoon talking. I know how you young people are. Why don't you start with those daisies over there," she said pointing to the far side of the garden. "I will have the boys do the rose bushes. It really hurts when we women folk get a thorn in one of our delicate hands."

Mary curtsied before heading to the place indicated. The entire time she wondered what she would use in place of a hoe. Surely they had some tools to help with the gardening. When she looked toward Katherine she only shrugged her shoulders. *I guess she has no idea what I am talking about,* Mary thought. She watched to see where Katherine had been sent and how she would go about taking care of the weed problem. Much to her horror Katherine ended up clear across the garden from her. Once she realized there would be no way to even talk or see Katherine she decided she would just do the best she could with her own hands.

She signed with relief as John and Richard appeared. Mary had a hard time stifling the laugh that threatened when they also got sent to different parts of the rose garden. At least, they had been given something to help them with their work.

Mary had plenty of time to let her thoughts wander. She felt disappointed because they wouldn't have a chance to even search for the secret passageway today, but she felt a calm feeling when she realized their conquest would soon be over. It wouldn't be long before she would be back in the arms of her mom and dad. *Why did I wait so long before praying,* she wondered. *I guess being so far away from home and not having mom and dad there to remind me I just forgot. I'm never going to forget again.*

Her eyes continually looked to see what her brother and friends were doing. She still couldn't believe that Katherine's mother had separated them. Of course, it shouldn't have been a surprise because it is exactly what her mom would have done. *Mothers must all be alike,* Mary thought. She started thinking about home, and then found herself rubbing tears from her face. *Oh stop it Mary,* she scolded herself. *Don't let anyone else see you crying, or they'll think you're just a baby.*

Despite her anger, the afternoon did pass quite quickly and soon the countess told them they should all prepare for the evening meal. Mary stood and brushed the dirt from her hands and clothes. She looked at all the others and realized they had been as miserable as she had been. She smiled, grateful that this was over and hoped she could avoid this task in the future.

John looked as though he would like to say something, but he held his tongue. Mary smiled, and he just glared at her. Then he held his hand out to her and showed her the blisters and also a thorn stuck in his hand. "Oh no," Mary said. "I'm sorry you got hurt."

"What is wrong," Katherine asked.

"Oh, it's nothing," John said.

Mary knew he didn't want Katherine to think he was a baby, so he hid his hand behind his back. He wanted Katherine to like him, and wanted to appear to be a big macho man around her.

"Let me see it," Katherine insisted.

John reluctantly held his hand out so she could see the thorn.

"I think we need to have one of the servants look at it," Katherine said.

"Oh, no," John said pulling his hand back. "I'll be able to get it out with my pocketknife."

"Are you sure," Katherine said taking John's hand into hers.

John turned bright red, and said, "I will be fine."

"If you are sure," Katherine said. "Otherwise I will tell my mother."

"NO!" John insisted. "I'll be alright."

They all followed the countess inside and then went to their separate rooms to prepare for the evening meal. The next time Mary saw John he looked much better, but at dinner she could tell he had an awful time holding his fork. "Did you remove the thorn," Katherine asked.

John nodded and then turned to talk with Richard. Mary shrugged her shoulders. Katherine still looked concerned, but since John ignored her, she decided she would ignore him. Mary thought it a stupid game, but she had seen people do that before. She hoped that tonight would be another fun night. One to remember. She turned toward Katherine and asked, "How often do you have entertainment in the evening?"

"Usually only when father is entertaining someone. Why?"

"I hoped that we could do something fun before leaving."

That was definitely the wrong thing to say. Katherine's lips puckered and Mary could tell that she had a hard time to keep from crying. "If mother knew you were leaving she would have had a party for you. Shall I tell her?" Katherine asked.

"No, you can't do that. What if it doesn't work out and we can't leave yet."

Katherine nodded. "I will not tell her, but then we cannot have a party. The four of us will just have to be content celebrating together."

"What do you mean?" Mary asked.

"Richard and I have snuck out before."

"Really?"

"Yes, but there is not much to do around here, we usually just go horseback riding in the moonlight, or something like that."

"That sounds fun," Mary said. "Do you think we could do that?"

Mary could hardly wait for the rest of the castle to settle down for the night. She hadn't been riding at night for a long time.

Chapter Twenty One – It's a Ghost

The four of them crept down the stairs and slipped out to the stable. Mary looked for the horse that she had last ridden and put the saddle and reins on her. When they were all ready to go, Mary and John followed the other two toward the river. Mary felt happy to think they would ride toward the river because other than the gardens it was her favorite place on the grounds of the castle.

Inside her favorite place to visit was the music room. In there she felt at peace and loved to play the new instrument, the rebec. At home, she never felt that way. Actually, she bulked at practicing.

Mary's mind continued to drift back home. She started to miss her friend, Kathy, and all the many conveniences such as talking on the phone. She almost wished she could go to school because then she would be able to share with everyone all of the incredible experiences she had been having, but first she had to get home.

Up ahead everyone else got off their horses and walked to the edge of the water. Mary followed them, and noticed the moon high in the sky. It was hanging over the river as though it had a string attached. John and Katherine disappeared behind a tree and Mary hoped they weren't doing what she thought they were. John wasn't old enough to have a serious girl friend. She felt nervous because that left her alone with Richard. She sat down on the bank of the river, and soon Richard sat beside her. He tried to take her hand, but she quickly folded it in her lap. She had no idea how to talk to a boy and so she didn't say anything. Richard cleared his throat. "It is a beautiful night," he said.

"Yes, it is."

"Katherine says you are going back tomorrow."

"Yes, we are. That is if everything works out okay," Mary said.

"I will miss you," Richard said.

Now what would Mary say? If she said she would miss him, he would think that she liked him. Well, she does like him, but only as a friend. Because she didn't know what to say she remained quiet. Richard cleared his throat again. "Will you miss me?" he asked.

"I will miss being here at the castle. It has been a fun adventure, but I will also be glad to see my mom and dad again. My mother and I are really close, and I can hardly wait to see her."

"I see," Richard seemed disappointed. "It has been fun having you and your brother here. I cannot remember when I last had such a good time."

It didn't take long for Katherine and John to come back and then the four of them once again rounded up their horses. This time they all rode their horses slowly back toward the castle. Mary knew the others felt just as reluctant as she to end the night.

Back in the barn, Richard helped Mary down from her horse, and immediately took her into his arms. Mary couldn't help the feeling that came over her, but instinct made her push away from him, a bit ruffled from being so near. After all, they were related. No guy had ever held her like that. It wasn't that she didn't like the way it felt, because she did, but she knew that this relationship could go nowhere.

After bedding down the horses, they all went inside knowing that morning would be coming soon. Mary stayed close to Katherine and tried her best to ignore Richard. As soon as they neared the room, she quickly slipped inside leaving the others to say their goodnights.

Mary woke up just before midnight. This time she felt cold although it was summer and she had a blanket covering her. She had learned a long time ago that the castle could be drafty and the evenings very cool. A creepy feeling crawled up her back. She had chills, and felt frightened. Then she heard it again. A little girl cried. Mary sat up, and this time she could see her. Mary's first thoughts were, *It's a g...g...ghost!*

The little girl walked closer to Mary, and closer. She was small, with ragged clothing, and she sniffled. Mary felt sorry for her, but didn't dare reach out to touch her. Finally, Mary whispered, "What's wrong?"

The girl didn't answer, but she again headed out of the room and straight for the spiral staircase. Mary reached for her flashlight and followed. This time she hoped that no one would bother them and she would be able to find out why the girl kept crying. Mary carefully tried to not make any noise, and she held the light close to her body so that she could just barely see. She didn't want to disturb anyone. At the bottom of the stairs, she turned to the left and walked straight ahead.

The girl took Mary places she had never been before although Mary thought that she and John had explored every inch of this place. When Mary thought, they could go no further the girl disappeared. Mary looked all around and finally found a small hole that she could just barely squeeze through. When John and Mary had come this way, they didn't see this small entryway. The young girl ghost waited for Mary on the other side of the wall. When she saw that Mary still followed her, she floated through the air toward a stairway. "Where are we?" Mary whispered.

The girl didn't answer, but motioned for Mary to follow. By now, the girl had stopped crying and wanted Mary to follow her. Upstairs, Mary realized it was a bedroom. She had an eerie feeling that she had been here before, and her heart almost stopped as she waited for the groans and mutterings to start again.

This was the way to the tower that she and John had gone to before she had slipped and they had found themselves in the Warwick Castle tunnel. She listened, but she couldn't hear any voices. Mary followed the little girl a little further and then asked her, "What is your name?"

The ghost didn't answer her, but motioned for her to follow. "I have been here before, haven't I?" Mary asked.

The girl nodded her head, and put her finger to her lips urging Mary to be quiet. Mary nodded and followed. Once she was inside the room Mary looked for the youngster, but couldn't see her. "Where did you go?" Mary called. "Please don't leave me alone."

Mary shined the flashlight all around the room. Then she saw where she had tripped. It came to her as clear as day that this was the way home. "Thank you," Mary whispered. "Now, what can I do to help you?"

The little girl smiled and waved goodbye. Mary waited hoping the girl would return, but she didn't. After a long time Mary decided she needed to get back to bed so that she could get some sleep. Tomorrow would be a busy day. It was also going to be a sad and a happy day. She wanted to tell John about her adventure but knew he would be unhappy if she woke him. Mary carefully made her way down the steep stairs and through the tiny hole in the wall.

She made sure she marked the entrance with a scratch from her flashlight. She wondered if John would even be able to get through the hole, but decided she would worry about that tomorrow.

Once in bed she had a difficult time falling to sleep. She worried about the small girl and hoped she would be okay. *I wonder why she kept crying. Maybe she just felt sad and was trying to help me.*

The mystery of why the youngster kept crying would have to wait because Mary really needed to get some sleep. She buried her head deep in the pillow and started to count sheep. She had to get some shuteye. Morning time came too soon and Mary didn't want to wake up. Katherine shook her many times, and then said, "I am going to leave you if you do not get up."

Mary grumbled and turned over. "But I'm so tired."

"You got as much sleep as I did. Now get up. I am hungry."

"I was awake most of the night," Mary said.

"Why?" Katherine asked.

"Do you mean to tell me that you didn't hear the little girl crying?"

"No. There is no little girl here."

"Yes there is. She wanders the castle every night crying. I have heard her almost every night since I have been here. I can't believe you don't hear her," Mary said as she pulled herself to a sitting position. "She never did talk to me, but she showed me how to go home."

"But we already know how to get you home," Katherine said.

"No, that is not the right way."

"Are you sure?"

"Yes, I saw the place last night where John and I stood just before I slipped and fell," Mary said.

"Let's go tell the others."

"No, we need to get ready to go eat," Mary said pulling her night clothes off and reaching for her backpack.

"What are you going to do?" Katherine asked.

"I'm getting ready to go home."

"But you cannot do that. When we go down to eat everyone will stare at you."

"Oh, you are right," Mary said.

She put her bag on the floor and stood up and dressed in the usual clothing of the fourteenth century. She took extra care in brushing her hair, and she did pull a ponytail holder out of her bag and fixed her hair the way it had been when she first came to the castle. Katherine frowned, but didn't say anything as she watched Mary fix her hair.

"Your hair is lovely," Katherine said.

"No, it's just plain old brown hair with red highlights."

"But, it is so long. Did you tell me earlier that you call that style a pony tail?

"Yes, that is what it's called."

Katherine laughed. "It really does look like a pony's tail. My mother would be really upset if I tried to wear my hair like that."

Mary reached into her bag and pulled out another holder and handed it to Katherine. "After I'm gone you can fix your hair this way, but wait until I'm gone. I don't want your mother getting mad at me."

"Is it hard to do," Katherine asked.

"No, just brush your hair all back like I did and then just put the holder around all the bunched up hair. I love wearing my hair this way in the summer. It's much cooler."

Katherine nodded. "Thank you. Mary you are truly my best friend."

Mary smiled and wiped a tear away as she turned her head.

Chapter Twenty Two – Saying Good-bye

After the girls dressed for the day, they went down stairs. "I wish I could slide down the banister," Mary said.

"Why?" Katherine asked.

"Because it's lots of fun. My grandmother has a banister that ends at the bottom of the stairs just before her kitchen. We all take turns sliding down it, until someone opens the door below and one of us goes flying into the kitchen. Of course, here it might be a problem. If you slipped it's a long ways to the bottom."

Katherine laughed. "I have never thought of doing anything like that. You really do have a lot of fun where you live."

Mary nodded. "Yes, we are very lucky."

Downstairs they found the boys already eating. John looked excited and Mary could hardly wait to tell him her story. Almost before her and Katherine started eating the two guys got up from the table and left calling over their shoulder, "See you upstairs."

"But wait," Mary called.

"Nope," John shouted.

The two girls looked at one another and Mary shrugged her shoulders. "Serves them right if they won't even wait long enough for me to talk."

"They are both in for a big surprise," Katherine said.

The girls took their time. Mary didn't want to hurry, and so they lingered as long as possible over breakfast. She loved the magnificent Warwick Castle with its secrecy, and mystery. It intrigued her and made her want to investigate more. She wanted to linger a little while longer and imagine what it would have been like to have lived her life back then. Would Mary be ready to pursue a romance with Richard, if she had lived in the fourteenth century instead of the one she lived in?

To her, entering the spooky, Ghost Tower had been a somewhat scary experience, but she was glad she had been brave and even though she and John had a hard time finding their way home she would always be glad she had come. She would cherish the friendships she had made her entire life.

"Well, I guess we can't put this off any longer," Mary said pushing herself away from the long table. "The food is wonderful and the company has been great."

Katherine followed her and the two headed up the long staircase. They knew the guys would be up another flight so they tackled it also. They both knew right where to go and it didn't take them long to find the boys. "How's it coming?" Mary asked.

"We haven't found anything yet," John said. "But I think we are real close."

"Good," both girls said together.

"Can we help?" Mary asked.

"No, I think we about have it," Richard said.

The girls folded their arms and watched the two guys. "I found the board in the floor. Now we just have to raise it up," Richard said.

After the boys finished and could look into the Earl's room below, Mary said, "It's too bad you went to all this work."

"Why?" Richard asked.

"Yeah, why?" John also asked.

Laughing Mary said, "I tried to tell you before you came up here that it wasn't the right place, but you wouldn't stop to listen to me."

"Yes it is." John said.

"How do you figure that?" Mary asked.

"Well, yesterday we all decided that it had to be above Richard's father's bedchamber," John said.

"That was yesterday," Mary said.

"She tried to tell you," Katherine said.

"If it is here, why don't you show me?" Mary challenged.

"I will," John said.

The two boys looked all around. The girls just folded their arms and watched. Richard and John knocked on all the walls surrounding the small room, and tried to push and slid the walls, but nothing worked. "Why would there be a secret passageway if this is not the right place?" Richard asked.

"I think they built a camouflaged door to help the Earl escape in case of an emergency," Mary said. "It's a great idea and one I'm sure many Earls have used it throughout all the centuries. Maybe even your own father had occasion to use it."

"If so, why hasn't he shown it to me?"

"Maybe he did not think you were old enough," Katherine said.

Richard glared at her. "What do you know about it anyway?"

Katherine ducked her head. Mary pushed him aside and said, "She might be right."

"I think since you rode to London to see him, he probably thinks you are old enough now. No father thinks his child is big enough. My own father wouldn't let me go hunting for a long time. He kept saying I wasn't old enough. Your father is probably just like mine," John said.

Richard nodded. "Sorry, Katherine. I should not have said that."

"That is alright," Katherine said.

"I wanted to know your father better," Mary said. "I had so many questions that I wanted to ask him."

"Like what?" Richard asked.

"I wanted him to explain to me about the family crest."

"I wish I could help you. I have not been interested enough to even look at it closely. I have only glanced at it once in a while."

"Sometimes it takes something like what has happened in your family to make you really care about things," John said. "I guess I should start asking my father more questions. You never know how long they are going to be around."

"You boys better fix everything the way you found it, and then I'll show you the way home," Mary said.

Both boys turned and stared at her. "You know the way home?" John asked.

Mary nodded. "After we have made sure that no one else can find this secret door and make sure we left the Earl's room the way we found it, I'll show you the way."

It took them awhile to get everything back to normal. John looked at his watch. "Since it's almost time for the mid-day meal why not wait awhile longer?"

Mary agreed because she wanted to take one final walk in the garden. She also wanted to be able to tell her great-grandma goodbye. John wanted to see the horses again and so they all went their separate ways.

Mary found the countess exactly where she expected. She carefully walked over to her and spoke quietly, "It has been so nice staying here."

"Are you leaving, my dear?" the countess asked.

"Yes. My brother and I have imposed long enough on your hospitality, and it is time to go home."

"My Katherine will miss you."

"I know, and I will miss her," Mary said.

"I hope you know that if you are ever this way again, that you are welcome anytime."

"Thank you. Please tell the Earl that I'm sorry I didn't get a chance to visit with him for very long. I really wanted to talk with him."

"I am sure he would have loved to talk with you also, but since I have no idea how soon he will be able to come home, you better not wait for him."

"I know. That is why we are leaving," Mary said. "Please give him my best when he returns."

Mary turned and walked away with tears sliding down her face. "Oh Grandma", she sobbed. "I wish I could get to know you better."

Next Mary went to the music room. She picked up the rebec and played every song that she could think of. *This is such a beautiful instrument. I had no idea they had such things back in the fourteenth century. Maybe if I stayed here I could be famous. If I would practice more at home, I could play better than I do.*

Knowing the time to eat had arrived she made her way to the Great Hall. At the doorway, she stood and looked around. The tables were beautiful and she longed to stay a little longer. There were so many people around all the time, and everyone seemed nice. What a beautiful place this was. Never again would she take her life for granted. This had been a glorious experience and she knew she would remember it always.

The talk around the table was relaxed, yet there was a different feeling in the air. Maybe they felt anticipation. Mary knew she could hardly wait to see her parents again. She wished with all her heart that she wouldn't have to leave Katherine behind, yet she knew her wish could not be granted. She hoped to return, but also knew that wouldn't happen. She was eager to leave, but at the same time, she felt reluctant. She wanted to stay, but she also wanted to leave. How confusing her mind was.

Soon it was time for Mary to show everyone the way, but first she wanted to tell them all the story leading up to her discovery. After almost everyone had left the dining area she told them all to listen. "Many nights I have been awaken by a little girl crying. I couldn't ever find her. Until last night, I didn't even see her. She would disturb my sleep about midnight every night since we have been here."

"That is why you have been so hard to get up in the morning," Katherine said.

"Yup. That's why. One night we got as far as the servants quarters before someone opened a door and scared her off. That is the first night that I talked with her. I really felt stupid talking to someone I couldn't even see."

"Sounds like a ghost to me," John said.

"Well, that's exactly what she is," Mary said.

"That is not possible," Richard said.

"That's what I thought, but last night I could see her, and she floated through the air."

"Were you afraid?" Katherine asked.

"Not sure, I felt more concerned, because she kept crying. I'm still not sure why. It makes me wonder if she just worried about me. She never said a word. Even when I asked her questions, she kept quiet. That is except for the crying. Because she took me down the stairs to the lower level, I was afraid she would take me to the dungeon."

"What did you do?"

"I just followed her."

"Are you going to tell the whole story?" Katherine asked.

"Sure. Every night about midnight, I could hear sobbing. Last night it became real cold and I felt chills and a creepy feeling on my back. When I sat up, I saw her; a tiny little girl wearing ragged clothing. At the bottom of the stairs, she turned left. I knew that John and I had searched everywhere, but boy was I wrong. Then she actually disappeared. I couldn't find her anywhere. I searched and searched and almost gave up but then I found a small hole. I had a difficult time getting through there, and John, I'm not sure you'll fit."

"I'm not that fat," John said.

"I didn't say you were fat. I just said that it's a small hole."

Katherine just stared at Mary and when she talked Katherine's eyes grew larger and larger.

"Once I got on the other side the small child was there, waiting for me. That's when I saw her float through the air. She still wouldn't talk to me, but she did motion for me to follow her, and she had stopped crying. Almost as soon as I entered the bedroom I knew I had been there before."

"Then what happened?" Richard asked.

"Nothing. The girl just disappeared."

"Do you know the way there?" John asked.

"Yes, and to be sure that I wouldn't forget I scratched the wall with my flashlight."

"That was a smart move."

"I thought so," Mary said.

"So are you ready to leave?" Richard asked.

"Yup, I'm so ready," John said.

"I want to go, but I also want to stay," Mary said.

"And I want you to stay," Richard said. "After you grow up a little more I would like to make you my bride."

Mary gulped. "Sorry. I'm way too young."

"I would wait for you," Richard said.

"Sorry, I really do need to go back home. I'm anxious to see all my friends, and most of all I want to see my mom and dad. I couldn't do that to them. They would miss me if I never returned."

"I'm sure they would," Richard said. "But you cannot blame a man for trying, can you?"

Mary ducked her head because she knew her face had turned bright red. She wouldn't answer that question. She knew she was far too young to make such a decision. She still had her entire life ahead of her.

"Well, Sis, I'm ready," John grabbed her arm and pulled her to her feet.

"Okay. Let's hit the road," Mary said as she walked out of the dining room and headed toward the stairs. She led the way down the steep stairs and turned left. John followed right behind her, and Katherine and Richard also followed. When they came to the end John said, "Okay smarty pants where is this small hole?"

"You don't have to be so rude," Mary said. "I marked it and you should be able to find it."

"Here is a scratch," Richard said. "It is not very big, but I bet this is the one."

John and Richard looked all around and couldn't see anything. Mary walked over, reached around a small corner, and pointed to the hole. "I told you it was real small."

"You got to be kidding," John said. "There's no way even you fit through there."

"Wait here and I'll show you."

Within moments, Mary had totally disappeared from sight. The other three children stood staring at the hole that she had disappeared into. "Mary," John called. "How did you do that?"

Mary answered him, but no one could understand her.

"Well, it's obvious that I'll never fit through there. Do you have something that we could use to make the hole larger," John asked Richard.

"Yes. Wait right here."

John and Katherine started to worry because Richard had been gone so long. Mary also worried and several times she came back through the hole to torment John. "I still can't see how you do that," he said.

"It's really quite easy," Mary said. "Why don't you try it Katherine?"

Katherine did try, and could almost make it, but always had to give up when she couldn't quite get all the way through. Mary got impatient and she really hoped that Richard would hurry. Soon footsteps could be heard and Richard appeared with something that looked like a pick. "Stand back, everyone, and Mary make sure you are out of the way," he encouraged.

She hollered out the hole, "Okay I'll move."

A few minutes later, he hit the side of the hole and made it larger. He hit it repeatedly. Finally, he stood back and said, "I think we should be able to get through there."

As they ducked their heads and went through the hole they could hear Mary on the other side cheering and clapping her hands. "I'm so glad you could come into this great big beautiful tower," she said hugging Katherine. "But, what do you think your father will do when he sees the hole you made, Richard?"

Richard shrugged his shoulder and said, "I think I will have plenty of time to fix it before my father gets home."

Mary grabbed Katherine's hand and pulled her toward the stairs. "You need to see the bedroom upstairs. This is an amazing place. Come on John," Mary said motioning the others to follow.

"I still can't believe you found this," John said. "Are you sure this is the right place?"

"Yes. Don't you recognize it?" Mary asked.

When they entered the bedroom, the room looked a little familiar. The rock wall certainly looked the same, and the floor was dirt just like the one on the tour, but Mary could tell that John was still not convinced she had found the right place. "I'm not sure about this, Mary."

"Why?" she asked.

"Well, I don't remember a bedroom."

"No, there wasn't a bedroom, but the room was small just like this one."

Katherine and Richard just looked at the two siblings. Finally, Richard pulled Mary aside. "What makes you think this is the room you were in?"

"Well, it was small just like this room, and the walls felt clammy just like this one."

"But most stone walls feel clammy," Richard said.

"It smelled like mildew."

"Most small rooms in a castle smell like mildew," Richard said.

"There are no doorknobs and there is no way out of here except through your cellar and probably a hidden door."

Richard turned around and inspected the small room. Mary knew she could be right, but she could also be wrong. She probably shouldn't get her hopes up. "This is the right place," Mary said.

"Okay, if you say so, we'll look for the hidden door," John said.

The four of them ran their fingers over all the walls, and John tried hard to slide the stone wall to the side. He was almost ready to give up when something moved. Mary heard the noise of the rock moving and held her breath. "Is that what I think it is?" she asked.

"Maybe so," John said.

Richard moved next to John and the two of them moved the stone away. On the other side Mary could see the mist caused by the dry ice, she could hear the scary sound effects, and girls were shrieking. The zombie chased the girl down the tunnel with a knife, threatening to eat her. Mary breathed a sigh of relief. "We are back!"

Neither Mary nor John stepped through the wall. They both turned back to their friends. Mary ran to Katherine and threw her arms around her," I will miss you so much."

"And I you. Do you think you need to change back into your clothes?" Katherine asked.

"Oh yes. Thank you." Mary pulled her backpack off and reached inside. She pulled out her jeans and slipped them on beneath the tunic she wore. She then managed to get her blouse on and handed Katherine the tunic. "Thanks for letting me borrow this."

John watched Mary and also took the tunic he wore and handed it to Richard. He never had taken off his jeans so he was all ready to go.

"Whoops," Mary said. "I almost forgot my shoes. Here are your slippers, Katherine," she said handing them to Katherine as she pulled her sneakers from the backpack.

John walked over to Katherine and gave her a hug and shook Richard's hand. "Man, it was good to meet you both," he said.

Richard looked at Mary, "Can I at least give you a hug?" he asked.

Mary nodded and after the hug, she hugged Katherine. Then she grabbed John by the hand and before stepping through the door she asked, "So big brother, are you ready to go home?"

THE END

Printed in Great Britain
by Amazon

36437055R00142